A School of Dolphins

James Norman

James Norman

A School of Dolphins

ISBN: 978-1725084933

James Norman

For Alice

James Norman

September

1

Still half-dressed, I ran full pelt after the bus. I was late so it had already been past my house, but I knew if I ran through Sawhill Park fast enough I could catch up with it at the stop outside Derek's house.

Derek is my best friend – insofar as he's my only friend. We met on the very first day of kindergarten. The other kids somehow seemed to know each other already. I got to Kindergarten late because my Mom's car broke down. Everyone had already partitioned off into groups. Kids were sat around tables colouring and scribbling and being kindergartners. The only free seat was on the table in the corner where Derek sat alone. I took the seat next to him, and I haven't moved seats since. Our friendship was built on a foundation of social ineptitude and loneliness. And I guess nothing really changed since then, apart from school getting harder, cliques getting harsher and bullies getting bigger.

Speaking of which.

"Oi Morgan!" said Fist One, as I ran through the gate on the other side of Sawhill.

"Where do you think you're going?" said Fist Two.

"Come back here, Alex," said Fist Four, or it might've been Fist Six, they're all so similar that they've almost merged into one giant Megatron of a bully. A bully mechanically engineered with the sole purpose of the physical and moral destruction of skinny, pale 17-year-old kids with floppy hair named Alex Morgan (and on special occasions, those named Derek).

Mistake #1) Not running the hell away from there as soon as they saw me.

Mistake #2) Not taking the Tae Kwon Do lessons my Dad told me I should take as a kid.

Mistake #3) Saying "What the hell do you want?"

Fist One did most of the punching, while the other 5 stood there and cheered on their Quarterback and Captain. Fists two through six occasionally threw in a cheap punch wherever they could find room. Fist One was smart enough to not go for my face – that would leave marks, and people would ask questions. He knew that I wasn't stupid enough to ever tell anyone about these somewhat infrequent beatings. Not hitting my face was his way of making sure no one else found out about the assaults.

When he was done, the jesters followed their King out of the park, chuckling and guffawing as he finished with a "welcome back, kid" and a punch to the solar plexus.

I did a quick spot check of my injuries. My clothes were covered in mud and grass stains, but I wasn't going to win any fashion awards with the outfit anyway. Jeans, check. Ironic t-shirt, check. My abdomen was aching. That was where Fist One, more formally known as Jordan Wilkes, seemed to have focused most of his work.

Somewhat uneasily, I walked on. I knew I'd never make the bus, nor would I make it to first period on time, but I didn't want to go home in the state I was in. A cab drove past and I was tempted to flag it down. I checked my wallet and saw nothing but an unscratched scratchcard and a few receipts. My Dad gave me the scratchcard a few years ago. I don't know why but I never got around to scratching it to see if I'd won anything. To me, the sense of mystery was far more inviting than the momentary spark of excitement when you start to peel away that opaque film of latex. I don't even know if the card has an expiry date. If I ever got around to scratching it, the prize, if there was one, may even be void.

Walking into class 20 minutes late looking like I'd just been hit by a bus wasn't exactly how I wanted to start my senior year.

Although to be fair, I could walk into first period ass naked and no one would so much as look up from their desks, that's how invisible I am to everyone at this fucking school. Like glass, transparent enough to stare straight through, but God damn breakable. It's funny how the only people who actually notice me are the ones that want to kill me. If Jordan walked into the class naked his asshole friends would high five and hug him in a show of homoerotic camaraderie that is somehow acceptable because of the letters on their jackets. That's what High School is like for him. In the land of the pigs, the butcher is king. Jordan is the butcher, and Derek and I are the proverbial pigs for slaughter.

Jordan's hatred and torture of me started in third grade. He was stood with a group of his friends – the beginning of the pack – another group of boys was throwing a baseball around between them. One of them, Daniel Marks, misjudged his throw slightly and the ball flew at Jordan and hit him square on the back of the head. He flipped. He charged at Daniel and grabbed him by the collar of his shirt. Even at eight years old Jordan was bigger than the rest of the third graders, and most of the fourth graders too.

Jordan punched Daniel in the chest. Daniel squealed in pain. Until that point I'd been watching from the side, just waiting to see what would happen. But when Daniel squealed I saw a situation that needed fixing. So I ran to Daniel and stood between him and Jordan.

"Stop!" I shouted at Jordan. "You'll hurt him."

"Back off, Limey," he said. And that was the first time Jordan hit me. He hit me because I was standing up for a kid that I barely knew. I often wonder how different my life would have been if I hadn't tried to protect Daniel. Maybe if Jordan didn't hit me that day, he wouldn't have carried on doing it for the next eight years. The first time it happened I went right home and told my Mom, who drove me straight back to school and roared at my teachers for letting it happen. Jordan was suspended for the rest of that week, but when he came back on Monday he hit me harder than he did the first time. It was my punishment for tattling. Other than Derek, I never told anyone again.

Somehow, Daniel was part of Jordan's crew now. He ended up on the football team which guaranteed his place by Jordan's side. I doubt he even remembers the day I stood up for him. Surely if he did he wouldn't just stand by and watch as Jordan beat me?

I was wrong to assume that no one would notice me slip into first period History. Richardson ("That's Mr Richardson to you, boy") saw me try to sneak in. It was odd to me that a person who hated kids as much as Hans Richardson would decide to take up a career in teaching. And if there was one thing that Hans Richardson hates more than children, it's lateness. We'd been sent our class timetables a week before, so I should've expected this. I should've just gone home.

I was allowed to sit down after a tirade of verbal abuse "If you can't be bothered to make it on time, then maybe I can't be bothered to teach you for the semester," Richardson said. I bit back my retort so hard that it hurt my lip a little bit. I was slightly damp from the amount of saliva Richardson had just sprayed onto my face, and my abdomen was in pain from Fist One through Six's 'welcome back' half an hour earlier, but I was otherwise unscathed.

Derek leaned over from the seat next to me and asked with a smile "So, how's your first day back going?"

"Fucking brilliant."

—

As soon as the bell rang at the end of Richardson's class I stood straight up and walked straight out, not waiting for Derek, not waiting for Richardson to finish his sentence. "You leave when I tell you to leave, not when the bel—"

I needed to get out of that room, I felt trapped in it. I always felt that way after Jordan's attacks. I walked down the mostly empty hallways, and wound my way to my locker the long way round, staring at the floor, not daring to make eye contact with anyone. The hallways seem smaller on these kinds of days, like they're pushing me closer to the people I am trying to avoid. I walked on the left side of the corridor, hugging the wall. In my school walking on the left is sort of an unwritten rule to avoid congestion and loitering, I guess. But it feels like just another way of keeping us in line, making us move as one. I walked into the first toilet I found and hid in a cubicle until I'd calmed down. I put water on my face, checked if any of Jordan's punches had drawn blood – nope – and sat on the floor and concentrated on breathing until I was ready to leave.

Plastered on the hallway walls are various academic achievements of students past and present. Photos of science projects, essays and reports that received high praise are photocopied, laminated and pinned to the walls. A book report I did on 1984 in sophomore year is stuck to one of the walls in one of the corridors – I don't know which one, they all look the same to me. It got special recognition because I compared George Orwell's "Big Brother" scenario to our school. It wasn't supposed to be written as a compliment, but the school took it as one, gave me extra credit and stuck it to a wall. I found it strange that that was a way of commending someone's work; piercing it with something sharp and sticking it on a wall for ridicule.

I reached my locker and entered my code. Sixteen turns left, eight turns right, four turns left. Out of habit I looked around to check if he, or anybody, was around me. The halls were empty. I thought this was strange, so I checked the watch on my left wrist.

"Damn," I muttered under my breath. I was late for class. I picked up my books from the bottom of my locker and started to rush off to next period. As I turned on my heel I ran straight into the last person I wanted to see.

"Morgan," he snarled.

I didn't reply.

"I trust you know better than to tell anyone about our meeting this morning, Limey?" Jordan asked. "As much as I would love another round..." He cracked his knuckles in an effort to look intimidating. It worked.

Again, I didn't reply.

Jordan thinks that bringing up the fact that I was born in England is in some way an insult to me. It's not. He acts like it separates us somehow, like it makes me worse than him. I don't see it that way. To me, the only difference between him and I is the way our voices sound. Plus the fact he's double my height and double my weight and is generally a lot bigger than me in every single way. Apart from that, we're basically identical.

"Are you listening to me?" His voice raised. My eyes were looking anywhere other than in his direction. Suddenly, his hands gripped my collar just like they did to Daniel's many years ago. Some courage fights its way to the tip of my tongue and I nearly say something that would get me punched. Again. Sensibility overpowers the courage and I say nothing. Of course, I say nothing.

We were the only people in the hallway, if he wanted to hit me he would have done it. My fear ebbed away enough to allow me to look him in the eyes and nod. That is enough of an answer for him. As he turned to walk away, the hand around my throat relinquished its grip and I could breathe again.

2

For the next few days, I managed to avoid Jordan and his mongrels without incident. I did this by using a carefully planned routine of blending into the walls and floorboards. A skill which if it were an Olympic sport, I would win Gold in. Except, no one would know who to give the medal to because I'd blended in so well.

I'd come up in some quite horrific bruises on my chest and lower back. Fortunately, I wasn't at risk of anyone seeing them and asking me about them, I sleep in pyjamas and it's not like I've got a girlfriend to see me naked.

The only risk of exposure was in Gym on Wednesday. Had I turned up I would've been forced to undergo the inhumane torture that is taking a shower in the boy's locker room. I decided there were more enjoyable ways to spend an afternoon than being ridiculed for my 'tiny arms' 'tiny legs' and tiny whatever else. I've always been skinny, there's not much I can do to change that. The Fists, on the other hand, were all built like brick shithouses, so they had no problem with strutting around the locker room like they owned the place. In fact, one of them does actually own the place. Kind of. His Dad is on the board of governors and donated a crap tonne of money to the sports department to get all new facilities or something. Of course, they're all football stars – Jordan and his minions. "Williamsburg High School Dolphins – Champions Three Years Running" read the posters and banners that are plastered on lockers and stuck up in hallways.

When we are supposed to be in Gym, Derek and I sit on the bleachers. It's ironic really that even though we hate organised sports as well as everyone and everything associated with them, that the bleachers next to the football field are our favourite place in the school. And it's only partially to do with the fact that when we should be in Gym is when the cheerleaders practice their routines (or whatever it is that cheerleaders practice).

The cheerleaders are, naturally, all stunning, and they don't wear much. It's odd to think that the school provided the girls with these outfits to wear. Some higher up in some office decided that 'barely anything' is an acceptable dress code for students of the school. Their parent's tax dollars literally pay for the school to provide their teenage girls with outfits that wouldn't look out of place at a burlesque show in Amsterdam.

The cheerleaders have their own clique, of course. And, of course, the cheerleader clique tends to click with the football clique. Just like every other school across the continental US, cheerleaders date football players, and football players date cheerleaders. Having a girlfriend or a boyfriend around here has nothing to do with love or affection. It's about having someone to show off to your friends. Not that I'd ever have the balls or the chance to try it with one of them. The closest I'd come was an accidental boob graze as I walked past Stacey Romero's desk in Science class. As much as I hoped she didn't notice it, her scowl as she turned to face me told me she did. As torturously embarrassing as that was, it was the first time she'd acknowledged me. And all it took was a boob graze!

The cheerleaders are pretty much off limits unless you're a football player, and the football players are pretty much off limits unless you're a cheerleader. That's how it works. But there is one exception.

The football team were training at the same time as the cheerleaders. I watched as Jenny Evans waved towards her boyfriend, Jordan. Of course, her boyfriend is Jordan. Fist One. The bane of my existence. The Bane to my Batman.

Head of the yearbook committee, head of the school council and dance committee, president of the fundraising committee, Jenny is the undisputed president of the everything-high-school-related-ever society.

Jenny is conventionally beautiful, as well as every other kind of beautiful. "Blonde. Boobs. Banging" as Derek has put it on more than one occasion. But to me it's not even about any of that, the thing with Jenny is that even given her position, her status, her boyfriend, she is completely and wholly sincere, wonderful and caring. I'm not in love with her, but she's the one person in that group that doesn't make me want to vomit. Yes, she's stunning, beautiful and lots of other adjectives listed in the thesaurus as being synonyms of beautiful. Her eyes are the difference though.

Her eyes are an intense blue. I get occasional glimpses of them when I see her around school, or when there's a photo of her in one of the school newsletters, but no photo can capture, and no computer can print how deep a blue her eyes are.

Jenny is always organising something, prom, sports games, cheer meets. This time she was organising the Welcome Back Fair. As I sat and watched her from my safe vantage point in the bleachers I saw her with a group of friends and fellow committee members, they were all pointing at areas of the football field and gesticulating, making shapes with their hands as they handcrafted a vision of the Fair. The fair was happening straight after the school day finished. It amazed me that she's capable of planning something so grandiose on the day we start back at school. She must have been planning it over the summer as well.

I've known Jenny for years, but she doesn't know me. Everyone knows Jenny, it's hard not to when she's basically the president of everything, and she always has been. In middle school she was the one that would give the speeches in the class assemblies, or hand out the homework sheets. We got the same bus home before she started driving. She has been an ever-present part of my life, and I've been a never-present part of hers.

"You haven't got a chance mate," Derek said, snapping me out of my daze. I had clearly been staring at her, and he'd picked up on it. "Seriously, never in all past present and future dimensions will you ever have a chance with Jenny Evans."

"Don't you think I know that? And anyway, I don't even like her. She's just... I don't know. Nice."

"She's nice? That's real deep mate. You should try telling her that."

"Shut up and eat your lunch."

———

Sometime between when we were supposed to be in Gym and when the final bell rang, Derek and I decided that we would go to the Welcome Back Fair. It was a yearly thing at Williamsburg, but for the past few years Derek and I had skipped it, not deeming it necessary to inflict ourselves to more pain of being around the rest of our class. This year was different though. This year was the first year that Jenny had organised the WBF. She'd put so much effort into organising it I figured I owed it to her to make an appearance. I didn't explicitly tell Derek that this was my reason for wanting to go, but he knows me well enough that he probably guessed it would be. He didn't take too much persuading.

"It's our last year at high school. We should probably indulge in some of the falsities whilst we still can!" I said to him during last period Biology.

Mrs Stillman was drawing an in-depth diagram of the human heart on the board at the front of the room. The squeaks of the calcium sulphate chalk on the black slate, although nauseating to the ear, when combined with the idle chatter of our classmates gave enough noise that Derek and I could speak in relative privacy.

"Indulging in falsities?" Derek said incredulously. "If that's the story you're going with then I'll take your word for it." He turned his head to the front of the class, it's possible that he was directing his attention to Mrs Stillman's gradually forming heart diagram, but I swore I saw his eyes flicker from Jenny to me and back again.

She always sits at the front of classes, yet we tend to sit at the back. I've always guessed it's because she likes to be able to get up and leave as soon as the bell rings so she can stride off to her next meeting or appointment with the school council or whatever other prior engagement she has that day. Derek and I prefer a seat at the back of the room. Sitting with no one behind us means that no one can see us, which fits in pretty well with our general ethos about surviving school.

Jenny was scribbling notes ferociously into a notepad, but from the way she was moving her pen across the page she clearly wasn't copying Mrs Stillman's diagram. She wasn't drawing, she was writing something. Probably an application letter or a speech or the minutes of her last meeting. She did this a lot, I'd begun to notice. She always uses this bright pink pen that her Mom must have given her because it has **"Mrs L. Evans Esq"** printed in black writing along the shaft. Jenny is beautiful and girly but she has this organised and structured presence about her. I'd gathered Jenny's mother was a lawyer because of the "Esquire" title after her Mom's name on the shaft of the pen.

I knew these things about her without ever having actually spoken to her, I just like to watch her because the more I do the more I find out about her. That's another benefit of sitting at the back of the room. I could look at Jenny all I liked without people noticing that I'm doing it. Occasionally I feel like she must know that I'm doing it, because she turns around in her chair, or flicks her hair out of her face and over her right shoulder to get a better view of the room. But when I can see she's about to turn, I just look away. I think I'd spontaneously combust in my seat if she ever turned around and our eyes met.

The final bell rang before Mrs Stillman could finish her drawing, which pretty much rendered the entire lesson a waste of time. Suddenly I didn't feel bad about not taking notes. As people rose from their chairs and continued their conversations at a regular gusto, Mrs Stillman tried to shout over the noise that she "wants the diagram completed as homework." But she's so small and frail that unless you're lip reading, her voice can't carry past the front row of desks. She knows she's fighting a losing battle trying to talk over people twice her size, so she slumped into her chair and crossed her arms, defeated.

The crowd of people dispersed through the classroom door, all jostling for the smallest bit of space to get through. Derek and I walked slowly to avoid the melee. Mrs Stillman looked my way and we locked eyes. Feeling sorry for her, I smiled. The door was now free of people so we left Biology and walked towards our lockers.

"So… what exactly will we be doing at the Fair?" Derek said as we walked down the hallway together.

"I dunno," I said. "Fair things."

"…such as?" he questioned. "All of the wonderful fair related amusements that you've been dying to try out since we started here?"

"You see right through me, don't you?" I said. He knew.

"Like glass," he chuckled. "Will she even be there? She's gotta be sick of the thing if she's been planning it all summer." He didn't even need to say her name for us both to know who he was talking about.

"Well she'll probably want to make sure everything goes smoothly or something. I don't know." I don't know why I wanted to go so much. Derek was right. These events never interested me before. There was no reason for me to go. She would be there with her boyfriend or her friends and I would be there with Derek, admiring from a safe distance, not speaking to her, only thinking about speaking to her, and making sure she didn't know that I was thinking about speaking to her.

We'd reached Derek's locker and he unceremoniously threw his bag into it once he'd entered the combination. I placed, more than threw, my bag on top of Derek's in his locker. He let me borrow it when we couldn't be bothered to walk to mine.

"To the fair," Derek proclaimed.

I followed him out of the side doors and towards the sports field, mimicking him in agreement.

"To the fair."

A School of Dolphins

3

We arrived at the fair and were surrounded by our school colours. Banners painted in red and yellow were draped from the sides of the bleachers. The school sports field had been transformed completely. The bare field was now littered with pop-up stands which each bore a different banner.

"Sign up to Drama Club" "Sign up to Debate Club" "Sign up for Swim Team"

There was a noticeable theme to the stalls around the field. Signing up. Of course, none of that interested Derek or me. We were just there for, well, we weren't really there for any reason. We weren't going to join any clubs, we weren't going to participate in the games or events that Jenny had planned. But it was obvious that she had planned the whole thing very well, everyone and everything seemed to be working in harmony. The biggest compliment I could give her is that somehow it managed to be the perfect combination of brilliant and crazy all at the same time.

Derek and I flitted through the crowds of people, doing our best to avoid either eye or physical contact with anyone else. There really wasn't much to do if we weren't interested in joining anything. I'd begun to think it was a bad idea to come when I saw something that changed my mind.

Jenny was walking straight towards where Derek and I were standing. A red dress clung to her skin and she wore a yellow ribbon in her hair. She was surrounded by a group of cheerleaders who were all wearing their cheer outfits, or whatever they're called. They all looked incredibly average next to Jenny.

Even though Jenny isn't one of the cheerleaders, they all act as if she is. She's the queen of the pack, and they follow her. She isn't bossy or anything, they just look up to her in the same way most of our school does. That's the aura she gives off. Just when I was beginning to allow myself to think that she was actually walking towards me she changed direction and walked down a row of stalls to speak to someone else. My eyes followed her.

"You can look, but you can't touch," said an all too familiar voice from behind me.

I turned. Jordan and Daniel stood facing us with their arms folded across their chests. Jordan was looking in Jenny's direction.

"I should probably break your legs for looking at my girlfriend like that," he said. "But let's be honest, you're not a threat to me."

There were so many smart-ass comments that I wanted to say, but all of them would guarantee me a punch. So instead, as usual, I said nothing. Daniel's eyes flickered between Jordan, Derek and me. He looked uncomfortable and out of place. Rarely had I seen Jordan with just one friend for back up. He likes to travel with as many of them as he can. It makes him feel safer. Bigger. My eyes screamed "I protected you!" at Daniel but my lips stayed shut. Derek's, however, didn't.

"Just leave Jordan, there's no point you being here getting in our faces. Just. Leave."

Brave. Derek had always been braver than me. When we play video games together, he's always the one to go in firing, whereas I stay back. Reserved. Quiet. A vein on the side of Jordan's neck quivered. His temperature was rising and his tolerance was falling.

This was getting dangerous.

He cracked his knuckles, either out of habit or for dramatic effect, I wasn't sure. Physically he's twice my size and twice my strength, which explains why I've never fought back. Even if I tried he would just swat away my attempts as if I were a fly trying to land on his neck. Jordan was staring at Derek, glaring, even. And all credit to Derek he glared right back, unblinking.

"Come on Jord," Daniel said, trying to defuse the situation. "Let's just go"

"Right. Okay. I'm watching you, Morgan," Jordan said, and he gave each of us one final glare with a simultaneous knuckle crack and walked away.

After the altercation with Jordan, the fair pretty much sucked. I mean, it sucked in the first place, but being threatened kind of made it worse. We wandered around for a bit after Jordan and Daniel left, walking up to stalls we knew we had no interest in learning anything about. We gave fitting in a try and we got metaphorically sent packing. Derek suggested we go home and I was quick to agree with him. We'd already outstayed our welcome. Neither of us had our own car, and we'd stayed past the last bus so an unwanted walk home was necessary.

During the walk home, I again found myself wondering if my life would have been different if I hadn't stuck up for Daniel in third grade. If I hadn't thrown myself in front of a Jordan shaped train, who knows, his hatred of me might have never started. We might have ended up friends. Jordan and Daniel did, after all.

There have been many, many metaphors written to describe high school: a pyramid, a ladder, a career, to name a few. But my theory follows something we learnt about in Math class. Decision trees.

Imagine a series of decisions, and for simplicity's sake, each decision yields either a yes or no answer. If you start with one single decision, from there you can either take the yes path, or you can take the no path.

With this first decision, whatever option you take you're not going to be too far from the path that you would have taken if you chose the other option.

At first, this individual decision doesn't seem particularly important. You choose yes or no and you get on with your life. But when you combine a series of decisions — and let's be honest, growing up is a series of decisions and mistakes, right ones and wrong ones — you get a path that looks a lot different to the first one.

It's like when you play campaign mode on a video game; you can choose to take different routes through the game, you can spare a life where you could have taken one. You can head left down a tunnel when you could have gone right. You can choose to play tactically or aggressively. Each decision you make affects the outcome of the story, and ultimately, it affects your progress and growth within the game.

Sometimes the decision you make will lead you to two completely different places, or sometimes you could make different decisions, but end up in the same place. There are probably dozens of ways of getting to outcome number five, you could take all these different routes and end up at outcome number five. You could say yes to every decision and you'd end up at outcome A, or you could say no to every decision and end up and outcome H, and your life would look a whole lot different.

But when you get to outcome H, it's almost impossible to make your way back to outcome A. Your paths have diverged too much. You'd have to unwind your path and undo every decision you made along the way to be able to get there. But life doesn't work like that, nor do decision trees, and nor does high school.

Once you've made a decision, you're stuck with it. And you can't go back. At any point you can decide to alter your path to get closer to where you want to be, but you can't change the path you took to get there.

The very first decision – at least, the first important one – of my high school decision tree was the decision I made to help Daniel in third grade. Yes, granted, the next decision I made could have led me away from the path I've ended up on – the path to this lonely, isolated, solitary existence – but it didn't.

I'm here now thanks to each and every choice I made throughout my own personal decision tree, and it all started with, theoretically, the wrong decision. But how would I have felt about myself if I'd ignored Daniel, and let him take the beating instead? How would his decision tree have changed if I hadn't jumped in and made the choice for him?

If I ignored the fact that Jordan was threatening Daniel, if I looked the other way and carried on with my third-grade business, then my life could be very different right now. I could have been someone different. My path would have had a different outcome, with different friends, and a different social status.

I could be opaque, but now I am transparent.

I could be red, but now I am blue.

I could be something, but now I am nothing.

4

Friday started with Charlie, my little brother. Charlie is completely deaf. He lost his hearing in Kindergarten when a boiler exploded near him. It was just after his fifth birthday. He got fairly badly burnt and completely lost his hearing. We got a pretty big insurance cheque from it, but no amount of money can buy back someone's hearing. Over the years, Mom, Dad, Charlie and I have all mastered sign language and it's become natural to have silent conversations.

Learning sign language was a struggle at first. We had to employ a specialist to teach Charlie, and us, how to communicate with our hands. It's a lot like learning how to speak as a child, or learning a foreign language as an adult. You start off basic. The alphabet, which is simple enough. Then you move onto nouns. Miss Debra, she told us to call her, would hold up objects or photos of objects, objects that Charlie would know, like an orange or a ball, she'd point at the object and then make the sign for it with her hands.

After you learn nouns, you can start to learn how to string them together in a sentence, and combine them with grammar and syntax to make sentences. "Orange" becomes "I would like an orange" or "Can you pass me an orange?" Of course, it was easier for of us with fully functioning ears to learn how to sign, but together we carried on with it until we could talk to Charlie as easily as if he had never lost his hearing.

Charlie is 13 and home-schooled. Mom does her best, but I can't help but think that he's not getting the best education, and that he'd be much better off at public school. But the problem is, private schools that cater for deaf kids are really expensive, and with Mom having to quit work to take care of Charlie full time, it became infeasible, even with the pay-out the insurance company gave us. Dad works his ass off trying to get food on the table, and clothes on our back, so we hardly see him.

If it had happened when we were living in England (hurray for free health care) the costs of Charlie's medical bills would've been covered. But we don't get that in America, so even though my Dad has worked sixty hour weeks every week since it happened, we're still paying off the bills.

We moved because the company my Dad works for got 'absorbed', as he described it, by this big American multinational conglomerate group or something. So, he had to pick up everything he had in England and drop it here in St. Francis, Kansas, U.S.A. It was twelve years ago when we moved – shortly after Charlie was born. I started kindergarten on the same day as the rest of my year group, so it's not like I was the new kid. I had been there from day one with everyone else. But from the beginning, I was an outcast because I wasn't American. It started with Jordan, who taunted me and bullied me about it for a while, relentlessly. He did it because he got laughs from the rest of the year group when he did so. When they stopped laughing it wasn't because they didn't find it funny anymore. They'd just moved on from it, and were henceforth oblivious to anything that happened between Jordan and me.

Jordan stopped tormenting me as relentlessly for being English over time, but he moved on to other things. Next, it was because I was so skinny, because I was so small, because my Mom didn't have a job. He always found a new thing to taunt me for, but he still gets in a 'limey' jab whenever he can. To be honest, he's so stupid I doubt he even knows what he's calling me. He probably just Googled 'racist things I can call an English person to make him feel bad' and that was the first result. The word doesn't bother me, but his intentions do. Somehow he found out that Charlie lost his hearing, and even then he had to get in a jibe. "If I had to listen to your fucking limey voice all day every day I'd want to go deaf too," he'd said.

When Derek found out about Charlie being deaf, he took it upon himself to learn sign language. Of course, it's a process, it takes a while to learn, it's not something you can learn in a day, but he mastered it like the rest of us eventually. It has proven quite useful to be honest. What may seem like a scratch of the neck, or a yawn during a test has often been a cover-up for a silent **"What did you get for 2b?"**

And obviously no one knows that we know sign language, because let's face it, who would we tell?

Having silent conversations without the fear of being heard is great, but it has its downsides. If Derek and I are sat having a signed conversation, and someone sees us waving our hands in strange motions, I'm sure it looks pretty odd.

In Richardson's class first period on Friday, Derek greeted me with a signed hello, palm extended and facing outwards from your temple, raised slightly into the air. A typical army salute, although his fingers were more relaxed, and they dropped, rather than being taut like a soldier's.

"So, last day of the first week of the last year of the best days of your life. How's it been for you so far?" Derek asked me verbally.

"Fantastic, yours?" I said with little to no enthusiasm.

"Same as, same as. Are you free tomorrow? Do you want to come over and play Quake?"

"No actually I have a date with Jenny Evans tomorrow night, and I'm sure it will continue long into the early hours of Sunday, so I won't be able to make it," I said without a hint of sarcasm.

"Seriously?"

"No, you idiot. Of course I'm free. 6 o'clock?"

"Okay," he signed, as class was now starting.

* * *

2:59:55
So close.
2:59:56
Almost there.

2:59:56

Have I really been staring at this clock for so long that I've actually stopped time?

2:59:57

Apparently not.

2:59:58

That would be a neat trick, being able to stop time. I could do a lot with that.

BZZZZZZZZZZZZZZZZZZZZZZ

Bell rings. Day ends. Week ends. Weekend begins. As everyone around me headed to their cars to start a weekend of drink, drugs, sex and house parties, I headed towards the bus to start my weekend of pizza, carbonated drinks and first-person shooters. I took a quick look around for Jenny, hoping to catch a glimpse of her. She's not too far away, walking a bit in front of me with a pack of Cheerfollowers. She usually parks her car on the other side of the road, so she'll be walking there, or walking towards Jordan's car, completely oblivious of the torture he put me through just 5 days ago. Of course, to her he is perfect. He acts it, at least. If only she knew.

She got out her cell phone. No doubt it's a text from him, telling her he misses her, and that he loves her. It makes me feel sick. He doesn't deserve her. She laughs at something, either the text from Jordan, or something one of the followers said. That laugh… that smile… the way her hair… Shut up, Alex.

Wait.

Fuck.

No.

She's distracted. She's looking at her phone.

She doesn't see it. Big and yellow and moving fast.

Surely she's going to stop.

Surely she's going to see it.

And I started running. And she was still walking, looking at her phone. And time was flashing by. Seconds passed in an instant. At that moment, more than I ever, I wished I had the ability to stop time.

She stepped into the road.

"JENNY," I screamed, and she turned to face me. And I was getting closer, and the big yellow blur was getting closer.

I dove straight at her.

"BUS!"

5

There are certain points in decision trees that are called 'critical points'. This effectively means there is a big decision to make. It's not a decision of whether to go to a fair or not, or what route to take to your locker, those decisions give eventual outcomes that aren't too dissimilar from each other. At critical points, one must make a decision on a larger scale, where the resulting outcomes are astronomically different. When I moved to America I could no longer continue along the path I was following by staying in England, for example. Nothing would ever be the same from then on, and everything changed.

Choosing to jump in front of a bus and push Jenny out of the way was a critical decision at a critical point in my life. Whatever path I was heading down, and whichever outcome at which I was destined to arrive, was completely changed when I chose the option that ended with me in a crumpled heap on the floor.

The weird thing about getting hit by a bus is that, and this sounds crazy, it doesn't really hurt. In the moment, that is. Don't get me wrong, I'm sure it hurt like hell, I just couldn't tell because 1) there was so much adrenaline coursing through my body at the time, it fought off any pain like an inbuilt morphine drip, and 2) I passed out pretty much instantly. An overdose of adrenaline or something, probably.

I make decisions every single day of my life, everyone does. I decide what to have for breakfast, what to wear to school, how to answer a question in class, to walk home or get the bus, to go left or go right, to speak up or stay quiet. In the grand scheme of things, I'd just made a pretty big decision.

It wasn't until four days later that I managed to piece together the entire story of what had happened before, during and after the moment I was hit by a bus. Various people had contributed various pieces of information that I'd had to stick together piece by piece until the jigsaw of my mortality was complete.

I'd been very lucky. The driver of the bus had seen that Jenny had stepped into the road and instantly slammed on the brakes. Unfortunately, a bus of that weight, travelling at that speed, takes a while to stop completely – you know, momentum and that. As well as that, I'd managed to launch myself at Jenny with such ferocity that the majority of my body was out of the way of the bus when it came past. The only part of me that came into contact with the bus was from about my calves down. It could've been a lot worse.

I could remember up until the moment that the bus hit me. It's the moments, the minutes, the days after which required some piecing together. The first part of the jigsaw was solved for me by Jenny Evans. She was there when I woke up in hospital.

Jenny was basically unhurt. She suffered a mild concussion from banging her head on the concrete as she hit the floor, and was slightly winded from me falling on top of her, but otherwise she was fine.

I wasn't as lucky. According to Jenny and some of the Cheerfollowers she brought with her, my left leg looked like it had been torn off, and glued on backwards. It was definitely broken.

Since then, my doctor has informed me that my leg wasn't broken, just fractured. Apparently, it was a miracle that I was not more hurt. "I guess someone was looking out for you, in the same way you were looking out for that girl," the doctor said.

After I hurled myself towards Jenny I passed out almost immediately, possibly through adrenaline, possibly through incapacitating fear. According to Jenny, when I fell on her she thought I was dead. My eyes were closed, I didn't seem to be breathing, I'd cracked my head on the concrete as well, and a trickle of blood was running down my temple.

Because it happened after the final bell on a Friday afternoon, there were plenty of people around, plenty of people that saw me throw myself in front of a bus. Those who didn't see Jenny there probably thought I was committing suicide. Ending it all in a swirl of yellow metal.

The ambulance came quickly, apparently. I don't know who called for it, whether it was a student, or a teacher, or a passer-by, but they got the ambulance there.

It was decided that the best thing to do was to keep me unconscious. Apparently, bones have a way of healing better if you're unconscious. They're not being put under any stress, and they get to heal in their own time. This part of the jigsaw was told to me partly by my Dad, and partly by my doctor.

My Dad reacted exactly how I thought he would and stayed extremely calm. He talked to the doctor level-headedly; he didn't worry, or overreact. Mom did what she does best and shouted at a lot of people, demanded their attention, and not really getting it. She wanted to know what was happening at all times, at one point she went up to someone and demanded that they go get my doctor, Dr Tilben, immediately. It turned out the person she shouted at was a very confused and equally scared coma patient who had just woken up from a three-week nap.

Charlie was quieter than normal – which for a deaf person is saying something. He stayed in a chair by the door, not making eye contact. I think he was scared that, what with Mom being how she is, and Dad never being home, if he lost me, he would have no one to talk to. No one to laugh with.

They operated on my leg whilst I was unconscious. Somehow it was only fractured in one place, and was an easy fix. Finally came the question of my recovery, Dr Tilben said that because I had been so lucky, that I would be able to go back to school, on crutches, in 12-14 days. I asked if I could stay off school for longer than that.

A hospital is an awful place, and because I wasn't in there for any life-threatening reasons I could appreciate my surroundings a bit more. Everything is very monochromatic in hospitals, the walls are white and the ceilings are white and the bed sheets are white and the patient's gowns are white.

There's very little to do when you're in a hospital, especially if you can't walk. There was a TV in my room that only showed age-appropriate, clean-cut and jovial programs. Crap programs, basically. A lot of the time I found myself just lying in my bed and sleeping. Sleep was my one recluse during my time in the hospital, if I was asleep, or at least pretending to be, no one would disturb me. I couldn't handle nurses coming in and out of my room every twenty minutes to check on me.

The worst thing about my room was the window to the rest of the ward. My room was a private room, it was just me in there, my parents managed to swing that somehow. There was a window in my room that showed the rest of my floor of the hospital. There were far sicker people than me on my floor, I was perfectly healthy compared to the rest. People were dying, their beds were emptied, cleaned and then they were replaced by new dying people. I felt like I didn't deserve to be here with these people, I wasn't going to die, not any time soon at least, but there I was, taking the bed of someone that probably needed it a lot more than me. I felt like I was stealing their grief.

Sets of grieving family and friends came and went just as quickly as the deceased did. I lost count of how many people died whilst I was led in my bed. Eventually, it got too much for me and I asked a nurse to close the curtains on the window for me. But when her shift finished and she went home, a new nurse would open the curtains when I was asleep and the whole process would repeat again. It was hell.

October

6

I had a surprising number of visitors over the 12-14 days that followed getting hit by a bus. Jenny brought her Mom, her Dad and, unfortunately, Jordan with her to visit me in the hospital one day. Her Mom, Leanne, swarmed me with hugs and chocolate and just said "What if you hadn't been there" a lot. Mr "Call me Steve" Evans just shook my hand a lot and stood very close to his daughter. Jordan gave me an "I owe you one", which stank of false sincerity, and stood in the corner, watching me.

I had a visit from Vice Principal Matthews, who said he "just wanted to make sure you're okay" but to me, it seemed like he was just trying to make sure I didn't sue the school. He brought with him Stan, the driver of the bus that hit me. Stan was very apologetic – not that it was his fault. "I didn't see 'er mate, and when I did it was too late for me to stop, then you come flyin' in and I didn't know what was happenin'." Of course, I didn't blame him, I didn't blame anyone, no one made me throw myself in front of a bus, it was my dumbass idea and look where it got me.

Jenny came back a few days later with a few followers, none of whom I had ever spoken to before. They reminded me of Fists Two through Six, not that there was any physical or logical resemblance, just the fact that within their respective groups, they were all exactly the same. Carbon copies of each other. They all craved Jenny's attention in a way that reminded me of a litter of kittens, fighting each other to suckle on their mother's teat. That image both amused and revolted me. Both times Jenny came to visit she looked incredible, which made me very aware of the fact that I was wearing nothing but a dressing gown. She had her hair up in a ponytail the first time she came, but the second time it was down over her shoulders. She wore jeans and a hoodie the first time, when she was with Jordan, but shorts and a loose fitting t-shirt when she was without him.

Normally I don't pay much attention to clothes, but the very noticeable difference in attire between when she was with and without Jordan said a lot to me, but I didn't let myself read too much into it.

Derek came to visit me after school most days. He brought Charlie with him, which I appreciated a lot. And, when I was allowed to go home, he came over as well. Those times with Derek and Charlie were the happiest points over the two weeks that I was bedridden, possibly overshadowed by the time Jenny kissed me on the cheek. When I was with Charlie and Derek, it made me almost forget about the accident, and what had happened to my leg. We would sit there, with my leg still in a cast, play Quake for hours and forget about everything that happened and ignore everything that was about to happen. Derek kept making me use the invincibility cheat, because "Even a bus can't kill you, Alex," Derek said. He renamed my character to 'The Hero' and kept shooting at me as if to prove I couldn't be killed.

Derek filled me in on everything that had happened at school in the aftermath of the crash. Before the 'accident', I was invisible. No one knew who I was, and that suited me fine. But apparently everyone was talking about me since it happened. I was the biggest piece of news anyone had heard in years.

"Alex Morgan: Hero of Williamsburg High" was the headline to the newspaper article the local paper wrote about me, a journalist came to the hospital to ask me some questions, but my Mom told her to "Fuck the fuck off."

Of course, once the students heard about this article, it spread around the school like the plague. According to Derek, every corner he turned he could see someone reading the paper, and frankly, he was getting sick of it. Because I wasn't around to take all the attention, it was all directed towards Derek, because he was the one person in school that properly knew me. He was the one that all the questions were aimed at, he was the one that had to tell everyone "No he's not dead", and he had to tell everyone how I was recovering, and when I would be back.

It's hard to tell, but as much as he complained about the attention, it almost seemed like he was enjoying it. People were asking him to sit with them at lunch, talking to him in the corridors, because he was the person in the school that knew most about the accident, the biggest thing to have happened to Williamsburg in living memory. My absence was making me all the more notorious; the school was not-so-patiently waiting for my return. I was dreading it.

According to Derek, Jenny had stayed rather quiet about everything that had happened. She was apparently unwilling to talk to people in depth about what happened, simply saying 'lucky' when people asked her how she was feeling. On the days she had come to see me, she had thanked me endlessly, as had the rest of her family. She would ask me how I was feeling, if there had been any updates or news on how my leg was healing. Whenever I asked her how she was, she would tell me she was fine, and not to worry about her and that "It's you we should be worrying about, Alex."

After two weeks, I could walk with the use of crutches, Dr Tilben suggested a wheelchair, but I knew I'd get to get enough attention, I didn't want a wheelchair to give them another reason to pity me.

7

My second first day back at school of the semester was somehow worse than my first, which is some feat, considering on my first first day I had been pretty horrifically beaten up before the bell for first period had even rung. The bruises from that beating had healed, leaving no evidence that they were ever there, but my leg was now in a cast.

It was Charlie who woke me up for my second first day back. He came into my room with a cup of coffee and a bagel. The bagel was left untouched and the coffee went cold, but the thought was appreciated. We had a silent conversation, which focused around him mainly, he knew not to ask me how I was feeling, or ask if I was nervous, he focused the conversation on his schoolwork, and told me how Mom was making things really difficult, but he was too scared to say anything to her. He joked that he wished he was the one that got hit by the bus, so that he could have a few easy weeks.

At one point in the conversation I started to fade out, as my mind began picturing what awaited me when

I got to school later. When having a signed conversation with a deaf person, it's best not to let your mind wander, because otherwise you'll have no idea what is going on. Only when Charlie got up to leave did I realise I wasn't present in the conversation. He knew I wasn't being rude, I just had a lot to deal with.

Dad drove me to school on his way to work, I told him I'd be fine getting the bus, but he insisted he drove me. My Dad has always been a man of few words, so it was no surprise that barely a word was spoken between us on the journey to school, as I was struggling to get out of the car I turned and told him thanks for the lift, to which he responded "Good luck, son." And with those three words, he had somehow made the situation more bearable.

I eventually navigated myself out of the car; I still wasn't used to the crutches. I'd asked Dad if we could get to school a bit earlier than I normally did, I told him it was because it would take me longer to get to class on crutches, but truthfully, I just wanted to avoid as many people as I could.

There were still people around, though significantly less than if I'd got there at usual time. I hobbled my way to first period Math with Mrs Greene, trying my best to ignore the lingering looks of the other early birds. I felt like both predator and prey all at once. People were staring at me, looking almost afraid of me, whereas I was stood there trying to hide away from their prying eyes. Derek knew I was getting to school early, so he came in early too.

"Alright, fucker?" Derek said, and he punched my arm.

"It's so good to be back."

"Ah, it's good to have you back. It's been a bit boring around here recently. After the accident everyone was hyped up and shit, but since then it's just been like we're all waiting for you to get back to liven things up again."

"Oh great, so I'm just the entertainment now?"

"Seems that way."

"Come on, let's get to Math."

We were the first ones there, of course, class didn't start for 20 minutes. Students started arriving in their groups, and I felt like Noah, welcoming all the different creatures of the land to my ark. In came the goths, the nerds, the jocks, the band kids, the cheerleaders, Jenny and Jordan, the AV guys, and the stoners.

"The animals came in two-by-two HURRAH," I signed to Derek, and he sniggered.

They all looked at me on their way in. Some gave me a sly glance, some physically stopped, stared, and then turned to their friends to say something. The last person in the room was Mrs Greene, I was thankful to her for not saying anything about my return, but everybody had already noticed anyway. On his way passed my desk, Mason Ford tripped over my crutches and howled. Knowing Mason, he did it on purpose. Anything for a laugh, with him.

"Good morning class," Mrs Greene started.

Not wanting to draw any attention to myself, I sat in silence, and wrote down everything that Mrs Greene said. At one point I coughed and everyone turned to look at me. That was a surreal feeling. I was used to being invisible, transparent, but right now I felt more opaque than I had ever done in my whole life.

The bell rang to signal the end of class, and if I could, I would have got up and run straight out of the door like my arse was on fire. But I had the crutches to deal with.

Pretty much everyone had left before I'd managed to collect my things. Derek had a class to run off to, so he couldn't stick around to help, whereas I had a free period. I knocked a book off my desk as I tried to stand up, put my bag on and juggle my crutches. I didn't even notice Jenny was still in the room until she came over, picked up the book and put it in my hands.

"Thanks," I said awkwardly.

"It's the least I can do, you did save my life, remember?" she smiled at me.

"I'm trying not to," I said, and she laughed.

Then we just stood there, somewhat awkwardly, me looking at the ground, her looking at me. Until she said "Well, I've got to go. I'll see you around?"

"Uh, yeah. See you." Then she walked towards the door and I carried on collecting my things.

"Oh, and Alex," she said from the doorway. "Welcome back."

November

8

For the next month, I was still hot gossip. Everyone wanted to know me, everyone wanted to know what happened, people who I had never spoken to before came up to me, slung their arms around my shoulder and spoke to me like we'd been best friends for years. It was a weird feeling, and what surprised me most was that I didn't hate it quite as much as thought I would. I'd always been a private person, so when people come up to me and invade my space it makes me want to hit someone. But after 17 years of no one noticing me, it felt good to be something, anything, just this once.

No longer did I feel like a ghost in the hallways, I felt completely solid. Present. A month earlier I didn't even know the names of most of the people in my classes. But after everything happened, I could walk down a corridor and feel like a character from a really bad high school soap opera, high fiving everyone and elongating names. Who I'd become is nothing like who I am, but much like the prey of the wild, I'd adapted to survive.

My leg was healing ahead of schedule. Dr Tilben kept telling me how lucky I was, and how it could've been so much worse. It's incredible that it healed so fast. Six weeks since the operation and I could walk without crutches. I still had to go in for weekly rehabilitation sessions, and it hurt a bit in the mornings, but otherwise, it had healed well.

I suppose it's not surprising that Jenny and I became close after the accident. It's hard to save someone's life and not have a connection with them afterwards. She's asked me to sit with her at lunch on a few occasions, and I accepted one time.

Lunch with Jenny was a strange ordeal. Jordan had a mid-day football practice so fortunately, he wasn't there. Jenny was nice enough to invite Derek to eat with us as well. We were a mismatched group. There was me, Derek, Jenny, Dana Jalofski (Jenny's best friend) and Cheerfollowers 2-6, who seemed to be the only people in the school whose names I hadn't learnt. I didn't know a lot about Dana. Her and Jenny seem so completely different. Where Jenny is more "Blonde. Boobs. Banging", her best friend is more "Brunette. Books. Boring." Dana is a tutor, and always has to run off to various appointments with various kids who are struggling with various subjects.

Dana was everything Jenny wasn't, but she was still a pretty amazing girl. They were similar in the fact that they both loved to keep busy. Dana was always helping people at the tutoring centre, or giving extra lessons where it was needed, and Jenny was always planning something for the student council. It was weird they were friends, they were an odd pairing, but they made it work somehow. From what I'd found out they grew up together and even though they grew into two completely different people, they stayed friends.

Because it was a fairly large group of us at lunch, conversation wasn't dry, someone always had something to say. Even though I had as much right to be there as anyone else I still felt a bit left out of the conversation, I found myself being talked over if I tried to say something, so I settled for saying as little as possible. Jenny always tried to include me in a way that the Cheerfollowers just didn't. Dana talked to me a lot, before she got an emergency tutoring related email through to her cell. She left with a "See you again, boys" and ran off in a hurry. I noticed Derek's eyes follow her as she got up and left the cafeteria.

"K-I-S-S-I-N-G," I signed to him.

His reply was a not so conventional form of sign language that included, and was exclusive to, the extension of his middle finger.

"You know sign language?" Jenny's voice startled me from across the table, she'd clearly seen Derek and me talking.

"Um, yeah. My brother is deaf."

"I've met your brother. He was there at the hospital when I came to visit you. I never knew. I'm sorry."

"Don't be. Knowing how to sign comes in handy. If you'll pardon the pun," I said, trying to lighten the mood.

She laughed. "So what were you two saying just then?" I looked at Derek in desperation.

"Alex was just saying that your legs look great in that skirt," was his helpful response.

"I didn't say that. Honestly. He's just being a dick."

"Haha. Whatever Derek." And with that, she turned back to a conversation her friends were having. But before she turned away I could have sworn I saw her blush.

"Aleeeeeeeeeeeex," came Mason's voice from across the cafeteria.

My growing friendship with Mason Ford was another shock. It started the day after he'd deliberately tripped over my crutches in Math class on my first day back. He was stood in the hallway watching as I dropped one of my crutches on the floor. He laughed, but it wasn't the type of laugh I was used to from him, it wasn't derogatory, it was sincere to the point of sympathy, but without pity.

"You look like you could do with a hand," he'd said, and walked over to pick up my fallen crutch. I didn't reply, I hadn't yet built myself up to that point.

"Come on kid, I won't bite." He placed the fallen crutch under my arm and put his arm around my shoulders to steady me. I tried to mutter my thanks. "I've got massive respect for you, kid. What you did for Jen was just… it was something else, man. I've never seen anything like it. I was there, of course, I saw it all go down. 'course I would've tried to help her myself if I had seen what was going on, but I guess I don't pay as much attention as you do."

He wasn't wrong, I do pay a lot of attention to Jenny Evans.

"Anyway, like I said… Massive respect." He removed his arm from my shoulders and continued. "You alright here? I've gotta shoot to class. You of all people know how tough Richardson is on late kids." I was taken aback by that. He must have been referring to the rollicking Richardson gave me on my first First Day back at school. I wasn't aware anyone was paying attention. Clearly, I was wrong.

I nodded to tell him I was alright, and this time I managed to say "Thank you" out loud. Somehow, even though he'd said a lot but not really said anything at all, what he did say had helped. Gradually, after that, we started speaking more and more. He was friends with Jordan, but he wasn't one of the Fists, and I doubt he knew anything about that whole situation. Most importantly, I trusted him.

"Masoooooon," I replied. Seriously, I was turning into The Fonz.

"Party at mine Friday night, you dorks in?" he said as he arrived at our table. When Mason called us dorks, it didn't make me feel as shit as when Jordan used to do it.

"Of course, we are," said Derek. "Where's your house?" He had obviously noticed it was 'dork' plural and jumped in to answer for us both. Derek was part and parcel of my friendship with Mason, any friend of mine was a friend of his.

"I'll text you my address, pass me your phone." Derek passed Mason his phone and we watched as Mason typed in his own cell phone number and rang it so he would have Derek's number too. "It's kind of an exclusive thing, so don't go blabbing about it to your two-and-eights."

Derek looked at me, confused. As his way of referencing my English heritage, Mason had started using cockney rhyming slang whenever he could. He often got it wrong.

"He means 'don't go telling your mates'" I explained to Derek, and he looked at Mason then back at me. We both knew that the only people in the world we considered friends were already sat at that table.

"We'll be there," I said.

"It will be good to see you there." It wasn't Mason who said that, it was Jenny, and then it was me who blushed.

Derek's hand signal came from somewhere to the left of me.

"K-I-S-S-I-N-G"

9

Friday came quickly. School seems to pass a lot faster when you don't actively hate every single moment of it.

The day of the accident was a Friday, and I remember walking out of the doors at the end of the day and judging everyone for being so excited to go off and get drunk and have sex at their little parties. And then I got hit by a bus.

The version of me from that day would me for going off to a party and getting drunk.

Previously, I'd only been drunk once in my life. Derek's parents went away for the weekend and he invited me round for the usual Quake session. Except, this time we broke into his Dad's liquor cabinet and shared a bottle of scotch. Although I guess it's hardly 'breaking in' if the cabinet is left unlocked. There's so much alcohol in there that we knew his Dad wouldn't notice.

I'm not really sure why we wanted to get drunk on that night. Probably some form of underlying teenage rebellion, or something built into the core of every angsty teenager that says if your parents go away for the weekend, you have to throw a party and get wildly drunk. Except our party was more of a small gathering; between Derek and me.

Being as skinny as I am, my tolerance for alcohol was far from impressive, Derek is bigger and could handle more than me, so when I was puking into the toilet, he was still swigging at the scotch. I don't even really know what scotch is, I just know that it tastes fucking awful.

I figured it was common courtesy to bring your own alcohol to a party, so I told Derek to swipe something from his Dad's liquor cabinet and bring it with him. I wasn't going to risk taking something from my house, my Dad doesn't drink, but my Mom would notice straight away if any of her bottles went missing.

Because this was our first party we didn't know what time was appropriate to arrive, so Derek and I arranged to meet at Sawhill and start drinking before we went to the party. This meant that at 10 o'clock when we turned up we were already pretty drunk.

"Well hello, good Sirs. How awfully nice of you to make it." Mason greeted us at the front door, with his best English accent, there seemed to be a good amount of people there already, so I guessed we arrived at a good time.

"What've we missed?" I said, struggling with my 'ess' sounds.

"Three fights, four blowjobs, two broken vases," Mason said, back to speaking normally.

"And a partridge in a pear tree," I said.

"You're funny, kid," Mason said, which was weird because I'm three months older than him, my birthday is in May and he was born in August.

Mason showed us around the house, made sure we knew where the restroom was and requested that if we were going to puke, that we did it in a toilet rather than a sink. He showed us the bedrooms and gave me a condom. "Just in case," he said. I very much doubted I'd need it, but I took it, laughed, and put it in my wallet with my unscratched scratchcard. As we were walking down the stairs, Jenny and Dana walked in through the front door. Mason went up to greet them and we joined him.

"Welcome, welcome. May I take your coats?" he said, the perfect host.

"Sure," Dana said. She chucked him her coat and walked towards the kitchen.

"Cut the crap Mason, where's the booze?" said Jenny, she seemed annoyed about something. She took off her coat and if I had let it, my jaw would have dropped. I'd never seen Jenny outside of school until now, so I'd only ever seen her in, well, school appropriate clothing. She was not wearing school appropriate attire right now. She wore a short black dress, tight like the one she wore at the welcome back fair. It was one of those dresses that has a translucent mesh covering the cleavage in a V.

We followed Mason to the kitchen and joined in drinking games that I'd never even heard of. The games had a common theme, which was to drink at every opportunity. Some of the rules made no sense, you had to always drink with your left hand, and if you didn't then you had to drink again, which seemed kind of counter-intuitive because you were already drinking in the first place.

Another rule was that you weren't allowed to call people by their first name. That wasn't too hard for me, because a month ago I didn't even know most of their names. Everyone knew my name, of course. I recognised one guy. Asmir, my old Chem lab partner. He moved to the US from western Asia last year. The story goes that his parents are oil tycoons that came to the States with billions of dollars. He immediately fell into the 'popular' (rich) crowd. Obviously. He was stood in a separate circle. Everyone seemed to stand in circles I beckoned to him from my circle to his.

"Hey, it's Asmir! The Saudi Prince!"

"I am not a Saudi," Asmir said back to me. "My mother is a Persian. You should know all about immigration, Englishman!"

"A Persian?" I said, still struggling with the 'ess' sound. "Like the Pokémon? Ha. What does that make you? Meowth?"

Immediately I wondered if the people around me would get the joke. Apparently, they did. They laughed. Everyone laughed, even though my joke didn't even make sense. Persian is not Meowth's mother in Pokémon. But still, they laughed. Everyone laughed, even Asmir laughed.

"Fine then," I said, raising my plastic cup in a toast. "To Meowth, the Persian Prince!" Other people joined in, and together we raised our plastic cups or bottles in a toast to Asmir, whose name was now eternally Meowth.

"Meowth, the Persian Prince!" My comrades echoed. Glasses and bottles and cups clinked against each other, and alcohol spilt and slopped over the edges. Some went in my hair. I knocked my cup against Meowth's, and we downed our drinks in one. Meowth left his circle completely and entered mine, he spoke like we were old friends and not one-time lab partners. When he drank, I drank, and when we both ran out we refilled them within minutes. Nothing I drank tasted as bad as Derek's dad's scotch, in fact, most of it tasted kind of alright. It made me feel warm and strong.

When the drinking got repetitive, people started passing around a spliff. A mixture of peer pressure and curiosity forced me to take a drag. I coughed it all up, but so did a few people.

Parts of the night disappeared before my eyes and from my memory completely. There were so many people at the party. At the start of the year I wouldn't have dreamed of being in Mason Ford's kitchen with Derek and Meowth and Mason and Jenny. No. Not Jenny. Jenny wasn't there. I wondered where she was for a minute before Meowth put another drink in my hand.

Mason's house was the perfect party location. For starters, it was huge. Like, really huge. Four of mine. And that's just the downstairs. Five of mine. Maybe. Five. Everyone was so busy and making so much noise. It was loud. Really loud. But I was quiet. I sat and I drank and I stood and I drank and I laughed. Derek disappeared as well and then I realised that Jenny was still missing. And my eyes went blank again and so did my memory and Jenny was stood alone on the bridge over the pond in the back garden and I walked over to her. She seemed upset again, and she was drunk, and I was worse.

"What's happened?" I asked her. The bridge over the pond wasn't much of a bridge, it was more of a little path that was raised above the water. I couldn't tell if the pond was much of a pond though, because it was dark, and I was drunk, and I couldn't see any fish. There was a water feature that looked like a waterfall that kept making a noise, and that was loud, and it made the noise of water dropping onto more water, and I realised that that's a really good metaphor but I didn't have the sense or the coherency to figure out what for.

"Oh, you noticed?" She looked up at me. I didn't reply, but I walked onto the not-much-of-a-bridge and stood next to her. "It's Jordan; you've probably realised he's not here tonight?"

"Well, yeah, obviously." I had been wondering actually, I was thinking that when she walked into the party. But then I realised she was upset and beautiful and I kind of forgot all about him. I'd forgotten all about him again now that I was here with her on this not much of a bridge over this possibly not much of a pond.

"Since the accident he's been really off with me, I think he got kind of pissed off that I kept coming to visit you in the hospital. But obviously, I couldn't just let it go."

"You only came to visit me, like, twice."

"I came a few times when you were unconscious as well; I wanted to know what was going on."

"Oh," I said. No one had told me that.

She shivered slightly, I offered her my jacket. "Won't you get cold?" She asked, but took it anyway.

"I don't get cold," I replied. Which was true, to me the cold is purely psychological. The human body is full of temperature receptors that send tiny little signals to your brain and tell you that you are cold. I like to think that I'm of slightly above average intelligence, and I'm smart enough to tell my brain to fuck off when it tells me I'm cold. I didn't tell her any of that though.

"So yeah, I guess he feels that you and I have some kind of 'connection' because of what happened," she said, putting on my jacket over her dress. She was covering herself up, which was bad. But at least she wasn't cold anymore, which was good.

"He's an idiot, he doesn't know what he's talking about. He's hated me for years."

I knew it was a stupid thing to say as soon as I said it.

"What's that supposed to mean? As far as I'm aware before the accident he never knew you existed. No offence." She was starting to sober up, so was I. It was becoming a dangerous conversation.

"I don't know what I'm saying, I'm drunk, forget I said anything." I tried to back-pedal.

"No what did you mean, he's hated you for years?"

I decided the safest way to control the situation was to tell her the truth. So I did that. I told her about the years of torment from Jordan and his gang, about how I would get frequently beaten, for no obvious reason other than to satisfy their amusement. She asked when the last time it had happened was, and I told her the truth. She sat there emotionless as I told her details about the times he'd beaten me, I told her about the physical and emotional batterings he'd dealt me. And when I was done a single tear rolled down her cheek. I resisted the urge to wipe it away.

The only thing she said was "I'm sorry." And with that, she ran off back into the house, still wearing my jacket.

My phone vibrated. A text from Derek.

"hHow yu feeligb!" He was clearly drunk.

I replied with a single word that summed up how I was feeling in more ways than one.

"Fucked."

10

I didn't hear from Jenny again that night. I saw Dana twice but she hadn't seen Jenny either. For the rest of the party, I was in a foul mood, I was coming down off my high and slowly slumping into sobriety. It wasn't until Monday morning that I heard from Jenny. I'd text her a lot over the weekend, just hoping to hear from her, just wanting to know that she was okay, just hoping…

She texted me before school on Monday saying 'Alex, can we meet at lunch? Just u and me. Jen x' I replied instantly, even though the use of 'u' kind of irritated me, and we arranged to meet on the bleachers where Derek and I used to eat lunch.

It was a long wait until lunch. I had to sit through three monotonous hours of classes before I got to be where I really wanted to be, alone with Jenny. Schoolwork has always been doable for me, there were never any distractions to prevent me from doing homework as soon as it was assigned, or studying for an upcoming test. Having no social life had its advantages, I guess. Things were different now though.

Recently I'd been slacking on schoolwork, and it was starting to show. Mrs Stillman dropped a marked test of on my desk.

"B- Not your best," she'd scribbled on the front in red pen. A 'B' wasn't the end of the world, but it wasn't the 'A' average I was used to. When she'd finished handing out the tests she took up her usual post at the front of the class and started drawing a diagram of the human lungs on the board, I figured that was a safe time to switch off and start thinking about what I was going to say to Jenny.

Her text was short and abrupt, and she ended it with only one x, did that mean anything? I checked previous texts from her on my phone, careful to hide it from Stillman's view. She usually sent two Xs at the end of a text. Did the fact she only sent one mean she was angry at me? Had something changed? What could it mean? Had I really become that into her that I was analysing the amount of Xs at the end of a text? Of course, the answer to that was yes. And I cursed myself for it. Before everything happened, when I only watched and admired her from afar, I knew I was pretty into her, although I never admitted it to Derek. But after spending time with her in and out of school, texting her, having proper conversations with her, I knew I was definitely into her.

She seemed to forget that in the eyes of society, we shouldn't be friends. We were just two people whose paths crossed in the strangest of ways. She forgot, or at least didn't realise, that before I saved her life I was nothing to her, and of course, she didn't know that she was everything to me. She didn't judge that we come from separate places and led separate lives. She treated me how I wished everyone would.

"Alex, perhaps you could answer that one." Mrs Stillman's shrill voice stirred me from my daze. I checked the clock. Class was almost up, I'd been daydreaming for a while.

What one? What had she just asked that I'd missed?

I'd begun to notice it wasn't just my peers who treated me differently since the 'accident'. (I still mentally give that phrase air quotes whenever someone uses it to describe what happened with the bus. It was no accident. I didn't accidentally trip and fall and push Jenny out of the way of the bus. It was full of purpose. Stupid. But purposeful.)

My teachers have also been different with me. Before things changed they would never call on me to answer questions, even though they knew I'd have the answer. They'd leave me to my carefully planned regime of being completely invisible and ask someone else, but after the 'accident' they seemed to think I'm willing to chirp up when called upon. If they're not getting an answer to their question they'll call on me. Maybe they think I'm just that type of person. That I'd take a metaphorical hit, and answer the question just so my classmates don't have to. The trouble is, as the test on my desk proved, when they did call on me for answers I more often than not didn't know the answer. Maybe I just had a lot more important things to think about. I spent a lot of time daydreaming.

I panicked, of course I panicked. I didn't know what she'd asked so I had no idea what the answer was. Her eyes found mine, expectantly. I hoped she remembered the time I smiled at her when she was struggling to control the class, maybe if I did it again she'd let me off. My mouth turned up at the edges and formed a grin.

"Stop grinning at me like a loon and answer the question young man," she said. "I said what…" and the bell rang. Every cell in my body let out a silent cheer.

I still don't know what question Mrs Stillman asked, but I collected my things and made my way to second period. On my way out Mrs Stillman smiled at me, knowingly.

Somehow, I survived the rest of the morning's classes and arrived at the bleachers 5 minutes before I had arranged to meet Jenny. I used to sit there every day and watch the world pass by. That wasn't even that long ago, but it felt like everything had changed completely. The girl who I used to obsess over is now on her way to have lunch with me. Me, Alex Morgan, five foot ten and a half, 130 pounds, it is incredible to think that anyone like Jenny would associate with me.

I saw her before she saw me. I watched her walk towards me, arms folded. I could almost make out the goosebumps on her arms. She has this habit of always looking amazing. Last time I saw her she was crying and she still looked fantastic. Today she was out of her party clothes and back into appropriately cut school attire.

She joins me too soon, I wasn't done looking. We sit there and chat, aimlessly and about nothing in particular. I can't imagine that she wanted to meet me just to have a chat. I figure there must be something pressing her, but I don't ask. Jenny is the type of person that even if the conversation is awful, you can't help but carry on talking to her. At one point we were talking about pigeons, and it was the best damn conversation about pigeons anyone ever had. It took me by surprise when she broke a momentary silence.

"I broke up with Jordan," she said.

Even though five minutes previously, I'd no problem talking about anything, I was lost for words. I had a mental debate with myself over whether I should say 'Good' or 'Why', but the silence had lasted too long, so in the end, I opted for 'Sorry'.

"Don't be sorry, it's not your fault."

"I feel like it kind of is," I said. And I knew that it was, but I can't say I was particularly sorry.

The silence continued, but it wasn't an awkward silence. It was a silence of two people who had so much to say, that it left them saying nothing at all.

This time I broke the silence. "How did he take it?" I tried to keep the glee out of my voice.

"Don't act so happy about it," she said. Clearly, my glee wasn't as subtle as I had thought it was.

"Sorry."

"Stop saying sorry."

"Sor—okay."

"I feel like a complete fool," she started. "All this time I was thinking he was my Prince Charming, my knight in shining armour, my Richard Gere."

"I assume you don't mean the Pretty Woman version, which would make you…"

"Hilarious," she said without humour. "I was completely wrong. After you told me what he – what you told me. I didn't want to believe it, I didn't want to believe that he was a bully, a tormentor, a coward, someone that could hurt you, hurt someone so – I don't know." Her voice cracked every time she got close to speaking about it.

"This probably doesn't help, but it wasn't just him, it was the rest of them too." I don't know why I was defending him, maybe something about seeing Jenny looking so dejected.

"That doesn't help, you're right, but thanks. I went to see him on Saturday," she continued. "I confronted him, and I wanted him to deny it, I wanted it to be a lie, I wanted him to say you were making it up. But he didn't. He just waited until I had finished screaming at him and he looked me in the eyes and he didn't deny it. He admitted it all. He didn't make any excuses, he didn't give any reason. All he said was that he found it funny. How disgusting is that? What kind of fucking sicko gets pleasure out of hurting someone else?" It was weird to hear her swear, she was so delicate and innocent, and to hear her curse made me feel uneasy. "Why did you never say anything before? Why did it take a mouthful of weed and a few beers to get you to tell me? Did I not deserve to know?"

I didn't answer, I didn't need to. We knew. We both knew. Before the accident I would never have spoken to Jenny, we were from different worlds, to continue her Disney references we were Aladdin and Princess Jasmine, two people living different lives, different in every way apart from a shared geographic location. She wasn't mad at me. I don't even think she was mad at him. I think she was mad at herself more than anyone. Mad that she hadn't seen it coming, possibly, mad that she'd been conned into loving a liar, a psycho, and a bully.

"He was cheating on me," she said. That surprised me. Why would anyone possibly want anyone else other than Jenny Evans? And why would the one person in the world that had Jenny Evans want anyone else? It didn't make any sense to me.

All I could reply was "Who with?"

"Stacey Romero." Of course. Head cheerleader and the captain of the football team. It was almost too cliché. I didn't know much about Stacey, she seemed a nice enough girl. Sure, she was attractive, but she was nothing compared to Jenny. No one was, in my eyes.

I waited a while for her to say something, but she seemed too transfixed on something in the distance to start a conversation. But I waited. By the time she started speaking again, I had almost forgotten what I was waiting for.

"Crazy, isn't it? How before the accident we were living two separate lives, two parallel lines that never crossed. They just kept going in their own directions. And now we're intertwined in a way that I could have never imagined." Her metaphor hurt me a little bit, but it wasn't wrong.

"Is Jordan mad?" I asked, avoiding what she said.

"I'm sure he'll get over it." Her reply was nonchalant but she wasn't the one that would have to deal with his inevitable backlash.

December

11

In the two months after I got hit by a rather large and extremely metal bus, I experienced a lot of firsts. My first high school party, my first joint, the first time I was on the front page of the school paper, and a lot of firsts in relation to my friendship with Jenny. Since eating lunch on the bleachers with Jenny there had been less backlash than I'd expected. I mean, Jordan and I aren't exactly the best of friends, he still looks at me like he wants to murder me, he just hasn't murdered me yet.

After the string of firsts came a lot of seconds. My second high school party, my second joint, the second time I drunkenly puked into a bathtub.

Second times are followed by third times, third times are followed by fourths, and after that, it becomes more of a habit than an occasion. But during this string of thirds and fourths, occasionally a new 'first' came along to spice things up a bit. It was during one of Mason's parties, a particularly wild one, and the first one that Jenny had been to since the time I told her the truth about Jordan. Once again we found ourselves sat on the bridge over the pond in Mason's backyard, but this time we were both sat down. We were having one of those conversations where we were talking about absolutely nothing interesting and we were laughing at and with each other.

We were drunk, but not as bad as the last time we were here. For some reason I was inspecting the unscratched-card I keep in my wallet. I was just folding it and unfolding it, rubbing my thumb over the latex film, being careful not to scratch any off. She noticed me playing with it and asked me about it, I told her what it represents to me. That I try to embrace the unknown, that the uncertainty attracts me more than the chance of winning. Her response surprised me.

"That's so romantic," she said.

Personally, I'd never thought of it as romantic at all. It wasn't a romantic notion in any way, I don't even know what it was supposed to represent anymore. I keep it unscratched out of habit more than anything now. It was just a piece of card that my Dad bought for 2 dollars from a Gas N Go when I was 14 because he needed change from a $20 bill.

In 2011 a winning lottery ticket of $77 Million went unclaimed, the ticket was sold to a Georgian resident, but no more is known. That ticket could've been put through the wash, it could be somewhere in a trash can, it could be down the back of a couch. Even if the ticket was ever found, it would've expired. The money would've been reinvested into lottery funding. A year later in California, a woman claimed her $23 million jackpot 23 days before the 180 day expiry time elapsed. The ticket had been gathering dust in her car for 5 months. She only bothered to look for it when she was reading a newspaper article and saw a picture of herself taken from a surveillance camera at the store where she bought the ticket. Lotto Officials had hunted her down to make sure the money went to its rightful owner.

The maximum jackpot on my scratch card is $100,000; tiny in comparison, and not at all romantic.

"Look what I found," I said, putting the unscratched-card back in my coat pocket and pulling out a bag of fish food pellets. "Last time we were here I couldn't see any fish, so I thought I'd tempt them out with some food I swiped from inside."

She laughed.

"It was pretty dark, you know... last time." I knew she was thinking about what I'd told her when we were last alone on the bridge.

"Is it weird that I want to feed the fish?" I said. I was drunk. "I mean, firstly I don't even know if there are any fish in this pond, and secondly, well, I feel that feeding the fish shouldn't exactly be at the top of my list of priorities when I'm standing under the stars with a girl that I'm in love with."

She didn't say anything. Instead, she stood up and reached for the bag of fish food in my hand and opened it. She took a handful and sprinkled the food onto the water below our feet.

"Now what?" she said. She was stood in front of me so that my eyes were level with her midriff. She was wearing a short red dress that I was beginning to really appreciate. I thought it would be appropriate to stand up, so I did. And I looked her in the eyes, and she looked back at me. And then I thought it would be appropriate to kiss her, so I did.

At first, she recoiled. She pulled back and looked me deep in the eyes, and her eyes were an ocean blue that reminded me of water much clearer than the water over which we were standing. She closed her eyes and returned my kiss.

As if we were dancing partners, I let her lead. I noticed that my hands were in my pockets, so I moved them onto her waist. I can overpower my brain when it tries to tell me I'm cold, but in that moment I had no control. Pulses were shooting from sensors to receptors, dopamine was released into my bloodstream, my blood wasn't circulating in its normal manner, it had a new direction and I was powerless. Powerless to my senses and powerless to the girl stood in front of me with her lips on mine.

I wasn't sure how long kisses were supposed to last, but I sure as hell wasn't going to stop it. I figured it would be best to wait for her to stop. Due to drunkenness and a momentary lack of blood flow my legs longed to sit down again, and I was worried that I would stumble and that we'd end up falling into the pond where there may or may not be fish. And I wanted to open my eyes and check to see if any fish had come to the surface and taken any of the food, and I suddenly had the mental image of the end of the Little Mermaid where the happy couple is on the boat and in the water around them they are surrounded by Mermaids and fish and I thought that if any fish had come to the surface to eat then that's what it would have looked like. And I realised that finding parallels between myself and the Little Mermaid should also not be high on my list of priorities when I'm standing under the stars kissing a girl that I am in love with. I could feel the corners of her mouth rise as she smiled whilst she kissed me; I took that to be a good thing. I'd not yet figured out the whole breathing and kissing thing and found myself thinking that having gills would make this situation a lot easier because you could breathe and kiss and not worry, and I realised how drunk I was because of how important fish suddenly were to me.

She pulled away and I could breathe properly again. I would give up breathing if the alternative was being able to kiss Jenny Evans non-stop. She walked off the bridge to the other side of the pond, the side farthest from the house, and sat on the floor. I couldn't imagine it was comfortable but I followed her off the bridge and joined her on the grass. I sat with my legs stretched out and after a minute or two of wordless breathing she laid her head in my lap and fell asleep.

My eyes skimmed over the pond and there were still flakes of fish food floating on the surface, but I couldn't tell whether there were fewer flakes than she'd thrown in so I still didn't know if there were any fish in the pond with the bridge over it. The water from the waterfall crashed down and I still didn't know what metaphor that was trying to represent.

A vibration from my crotch area stirred her slightly in her sleep, but it was just Derek ringing my cell from somewhere inside the house. I answered it.

"Look up," was all he said. I spotted him in one of the upstairs bedroom windows. I wondered how long he had been there, and resented him for it. It felt like an invasion of our privacy, but then again, I would need someone to remind me that it actually happened.

12

Jen-ny, Je-n-ny, Jen-ny, Je-n-ny. My heart pounded the rhythm of her name, a constant reminder that she wasn't some figment of my imagination, that she was a real, warm, omnipresent force on me. At first, I didn't know what to make of our kiss, and I didn't know what to do next. I couldn't ask Derek for advice, every time I mentioned it to him he developed a case of the giggles and demanded a fist-bump.

He was being deliberately evasive about how and why he had ended up looking out of an upstairs window in the early hours of that morning. I couldn't talk to my parents about it, I have spent my entire life hiding my personal life from them, and I didn't intend for that to change. Mason doesn't take anything seriously enough to be able to give advice.

Even months on from my accident, a lifetime since I was a loner in the halls. I'm surrounded by friends, yet I had no-one to talk to. Everything is different, but nothing's really changed.

In the end, I decided to talk to Dana. Part of me wanted to tell her just so that it would actually seem real. Like it did happen and it wasn't a figment of my drunken imagination. Although, another part of me hoped that she already knew, hoped that Jenny had ran straight home the next day and phoned Dana and to tell her all about the kiss. I hoped, more than thought, that to be true.

I found Dana, as expected, in the library. She was with one of her tutees, exploring a diagram of the human heart. Her tutee was a short, dark-haired girl from a few grades below whose name I did not know. I asked Dana if she had a minute to chat, but she told me she would be busy with Sahira for a while, but if it was important she could talk.

"No, nothing important, I'm on free period, just wanted a chat. I'll catch you in a bit?" I replied, and walked off without waiting for a response.

Even my last resort was too busy for me. I wished I could just get my phone out and call Charlie. He'd talk me through it. But having a phone conversation with a deaf person is about as hard as it sounds. I contemplated phoning him just to tell someone what I was feeling, the confusion, the wondering, the wanting, even if he couldn't hear me, or respond, it would've been good to just come out and say it. I was fiddling with my phone in the palm of my hand whilst considering calling Charlie, so when it started ringing I answered it in a split second, even faster because of the name that popped up on the Caller ID.

"Hey." I did my best at conveying nonchalance.

"Wow, you're an eager beaver."

"Huh?" I replied. Fucking great reply Alex, well done.

"Uh, just that you answered the phone really fast, that's all," I managed to mutter a somewhat coherent apology. I'd picked an awful time to develop mutism.

"Uh, no worries. Anyway, I wanted to talk to you about Saturday," said Jenny. If my heart wasn't racing before, it sure as hell was now.

"Oh right, sure. What?" I said. Not the most advanced lexical choices, but it was an improvement on grunting."I don't want to talk over the phone really" (then why did you call me? The sarcastic part of my subconscious noted.) "Can you come meet me? On the bleachers, like before?" She asked me, her voice soft.

"Yeah sure, let me just gather my things," I said. I wanted her to think I was busy doing things, not just sat around thinking about her.

I walked onto the sports field the way I always had, head down, and hands in pockets. I considered waving at Jenny, but remembered I'm not an English schoolgirl, or the Queen and so I thought better of it.

We stole secret glances at each other as I approached, not making eye contact, but not looking away either. An age later I sat down on her left-hand side, another age later she said "Hi."

"Hey, you" was the reply I had practised in my head on the way over, I thought it was cute and playful. What I actually ended up saying was more of a "Hyu."

"So... Saturday night..." she began, and she carried on without waiting for a response or acknowledgement from my end. That was perfect for me as I was still struggling to form words properly around her. "It meant so much to me. Just being with you there on that bridge made me forget about everything that's happened recently, like, the accident and the Jordan stuff, and I've got so much work to do and my parents are never around and everything, but just talking to you made everything so much easier. You know? Maybe you don't, I don't even know what I'm thinking. I've literally just broken up with Jordan but now you're there and you're you and you drunkenly told me that you were in love with me, and you fed the fish for God's sake. You fed the fish, because you're not like anyone I've liked before. You're nothing like Jordan, you're good and you're brave and you're kind, and there's the small matter that you saved my life, and I don't know if what I'm feeling is just because I'm angry at Jordan or because I am genuinely falling for you, but then you kissed me and everything just got so. Much. More. Confusing. You know?"

And even though I knew exactly what she meant, I didn't tell her that. Instead, I went in another direction.

"No, I don't know," I said. "I didn't think about any of that. I wanted to kiss you so I kissed you, it didn't require a lot of thought. It was more of an instinct, a reflex. Granted, if Jordan was stood behind me I may have taken a moment or two to think rationally about what I was about to do..." Jenny chuckled. "But I would have done it anyway. You're too pretty not to kiss."

"Smooth," Jenny said, and she chuckled again.

"Thanks," I said. "I'm not going to be winning 'best dressed' or 'most dazzling smile' at the end of year student awards, so my quick wit and unbelievable charm is all I've got"

"Would you like to win best dressed? Because I'm student president, and I could totally rig that for you."

"You could, but you wouldn't. You're too... Whatever the word is for someone who has a load of integrity, you're too much of that to rig an awards ceremony."

"Integrous?" she said.

"You definitely made that up!" I laughed. "But it sounds about right. I guess I'm not winning any awards for English either."

We talked about a bit of nothing and a bit of everything after that, both avoiding what we really wanted to be talking about.

Eventually, she got up to walk away and I followed her. As she walked down the bleachers she tripped and stumbled, I held out my arm instinctively to stop her from falling. She turned, kissed me on the cheek, and whispered.

"My hero."

January

13

Jenny suggested that to clear our heads we went on a real-life, proper date, rather than having emotional one-on-one chats on bridges and bleachers. Of course, I agreed that it sounded like a great idea. I suggested Tuesday but she had a student council meeting, she suggested Thursday, but I had plans with Derek so in the end we met in between and agreed on a Wednesday night date.

It wouldn't just be my first date with Jenny, it would be my first date ever. To say I was nervous wouldn't be telling the whole story. I was scared and apprehensive and hesitant and a load of other synonyms of nervous all at the same time. In my anxiety I did something that I don't often do, I went to my Dad for advice. Unfortunately, he wasn't alone.

"Just play it cool and don't mess it up," my Mom interjected. "She's a nice girl from a good family. Her parents are lawyers, did you know that? When I used to pick you up from school they'd be there wearing suits and driving a Mercedes and I'd be very surprised if their daughter – what's her name again? Jenny? – didn't go on to be a lawyer as well. They're both good at it. I was reading about them in the paper and…" she often went on like this. She was dominating a conversation by not even answering the question, a question I hadn't even asked her. I'd asked my Dad if he had any pearls of wisdom, you know, man to man, but she'd decided I wanted a more man to Mom kind of chat, apparently.

One thing that Dad did say to me, which helped a lot, was the same advice he gave me when I sat exams. He said that whatever the outcome, whatever the future holds, as long as you can stand with your hand on your heart and say 'I tried my best' then it doesn't matter what happens, because you've done all you can to make it work.

Jenny suggested that we go for a meal at this restaurant on the high street, Le Italiano. You could tell that it was an Italian restaurant run by Americans because any legitimate Italian would know that it should have been called L'Italiano but the owners went with Le without doing their research. Their mistake in naming the restaurant has been pointed out to them many times over the years, but they've never rebranded.

Even though I'd never been on a date, I'd seen enough TV to know what the main thing I needed. Money. I'd never needed an allowance until now so I'd never asked for one. If there was something I wanted, I'd wait for a birthday. Materialism was a concept lost on me, so money was never something that I needed, which meant it was now something I lacked. On the Monday before our date, I approached Dad and asked him if I could borrow some money, and by borrow, I meant have. He asked me how much I'd need and I honestly didn't know, so all I could reply was "Enough."

With a smile, he pulled his wallet from his pocket and withdrew three twenty dollar notes and handed them to me. "You're a good kid," he said. "Enjoy yourself. But don't tell your mother." Charlie was sat at the foot of my Dad's chair reading a book, but he saw the exchange.

"Why do you need money?" he signed to me.

"I have a date with a girl."

"A girl? What's she like? Is she nice?"

"She's..." I started to sign. "Extraordinary." I continued out loud, allowing Charlie to read my lips.

"Can I meet her?"

"You already have. Do you remember the blonde girl, Jenny, from when I was in hospital?" I said, and Charlie frowned. He doesn't like to think of that time, the time where no one would tell him what was happening and he thought he was going to lose me.

"The pretty one?" he asked.

I smiled. Yeah kid, the pretty one.

———

I realised that Charlie's description of her wasn't quite adequate when I met her at the restaurant on Wednesday evening. She wasn't pretty, she was breathtaking. I was waiting for her at the front of the restaurant, I'd managed to persuade my Mom to drop me off and leave before Jenny arrived. As Jenny drove past the front of the restaurant to park around the back, I caught a glimpse of her through the window of her red Chevy Spark. It was typical of Jenny to get a car that matched our school's colours perfectly. Through the window, I could see only her face and hair and immediately she looked different.

After she'd parked and walked around the corner towards me, I noticed why she looked different. It was the first time I'd seen her with her hair in curls. Each ringlet fell to just below her collarbone, and her fringe was parted so it almost covered her right eye. Black lines around her eyelids contrasted with the blue of her eyes and made them stand out even more. Her eyeliner flicked out slightly at the end, pointing towards her ears. She wore a loose fitting collar to thigh light blue dress. It was denim in look but not in texture, it buttoned down along the front and the very top of the dress was bordered with thin white lace that made flower patterns against her skin.

Her neck was visible, and around it, she wore a diamond pendant on a necklace that I hadn't seen before. The chain of the necklace was thin and looked like it would snap if it got caught on something. That explained why I'd never seen it before, I guess, it was so fragile. If it were around my neck, the chain would shatter from how fast my heart was pumping against my chest.

She took the last few strides to close the gap between us and when she reached me I found myself once again lost for words around her. Instead, I smiled and gestured towards the front door of Le Italiano. We walked through together and were greeted at the host stand by 'Mark', as his name badge read. I felt completely ordinary next to her, the Maître d', or whatever the Italian-American equivalent of a Maître d' is, must have thought we were such a mismatched couple, her radiating elegance, and me stood next to but slightly behind her wearing plain jeans and a white shirt I had borrowed from my Dad.

"Two of you, is it?" Mark asked. He had an accent that was definitely not Italian. When the restaurant first opened they went through a stage of only hiring people that could at least pretend they were Italian, if you did not look Italian, or could not feign an Italian accent, you'd have to look elsewhere for work in the service industry. The ruse has died down a lot since then, I suspect it's mostly to do with the L'/Le debacle.

"Yes please," I said, taking charge and stepping forward a bit so I was in front of Jenny.

"Somewhere quiet, if you wouldn't mind," Jenny added. The restaurant was over half full so the noise from customers and children and the totally traditional Italian music they blasted over the speakers made for a lively atmosphere, but Mark took us to a booth in the corner of the restaurant where we were relatively free from the noise. He gestured to the table by a window and asked if it would be suitable, I nodded and muttered thanks. Jenny sat down on one side of the table and I chose to sit opposite her, rather than next to her, a decision that I'd made earlier in the day.

Mark placed menus on our table, first in front of Jenny and then in front of me and asked if he could fetch us some drinks.

"Just a coke for me please," Jenny said. "No ice."

All I really wanted was water, but I didn't want to look cheap. I told Mark I'd have the same and he scuttled off to the bar leaving us in our corner.

"Hey, you," I said when we were finally alone. I wanted to tell her how good she looked, but I didn't want her to think I was only saying it because I felt I had to say it.

"Hey."

I did tell her she looked nice, and she said she'd never seen me in a shirt before.

"I'm going to be completely honest with you and tell you that I don't actually own one and that I borrowed it from my Dad. Is that weird?"

She laughed. "No, it's quite cute actually," she said, but I wasn't sure if she was lying. "Whilst we're telling the truth, in all honesty, how many of your Dads shirts did you try on before you picked that one?"

"Oh, I'd say just about all of them."

"Well you made a good choice," she smiled and looked down at the menu. As she leant forwards the necklace disconnected with her chest and swung below her chin like a metronome.

"Is that necklace new?" I asked. "I've never seen it before."

"This?" she asked, and grabbed the pendant between her thumb and forefinger, looking down on it. "It's actually my Moms necklace, she wore it on her wedding day and gave it to me for my 16th birthday. I only wear it on special occasions because it's so delicate and precious and I'm scared of breaking it."

"So this is a special occasion is it?" I asked, trying not to sound too happy with myself. She rolled the pendant between her thumb and forefinger before releasing it, letting it bounce against her chest.

She looked up at me from under her fringe and teased "Maybe."

Mark returned with our drinks and asked if we were ready to order food. I hadn't even looked at the menu yet. I panicked because he was waiting for me to answer, and I think Jenny was too, and I was glad that I'd picked a white shirt because you can't see sweat patches on white shirts and I was suddenly very hot.

"A few more minutes then," Mark said after a few too many seconds of silence, and walked away with a knowing smile. Jenny giggled.

"I'm an absolute mess, aren't I?" I said as he walked away. "I don't do well under pressure."

"I dunno about that," she said, and I knew to what she was alluding.

"Well, that's completely different!" I said. "But you're right, I'm fine when it comes to jumping in front of buses but when a waiter asks me if I want to order I suddenly freeze up. Funny old world."

"Speaking of that; how is your leg these days? Does it hurt at all?" she asked, we hadn't really spoken about it much recently. It was all kind of forgotten, because there wasn't a great deal of pain left. It would only twinge with pain if I moved it too fast or at funny angles. Rehab sessions were over now, and I pretty much just got on with it.

"Yeah it's fine," I told her. "Sometimes it hurts when I wake up but I barely notice it anymore."

"Good," she mumbled.

"What's wrong?"

"It's just that whole thing, it's such a mess. I am eternally indebted to you and I will never be able to pay you back!"

"Maybe. But being here with me is a pretty good place to start."

"Really?"

"Jenny, on the list of places I could wish to be right now, right here, with you, is atop it."

"I love that you can just casually use words like "atop" in a sentence and not make it sound pretentious."

"I thought I wasn't going to be winning any English awards, remember, Miss Integrous?"

"Shhh."

Mark came back and we ordered food, Jenny went first and ordered a classic lasagne, I wondered what the difference was between a Lasagne and a classic lasagne. I chose a chicken tagliatelle carbonara. He left and came back minutes later with complimentary garlic bread, we both stared at it.

"I feel like garlic bread is not appropriate first date food. Garlic breath, and that," I said, and Jenny laughed. It was either really easy to make Jenny laugh, or I was just particularly good at it.

"You know, you're probably right," she agreed. "But if we both have garlicky breath then it won't be as noticeable as if only one of us has it."

"Plus it was free. Two each?" I said. She nodded and together we ate the garlic bread, sacrificing our fresh breath. Personally, I'd gone through about a litre of toothpaste before leaving the house, looking back that seemed a bit drastic.

"You'd tell me if I had garlic flakes in my teeth, wouldn't you?" Jenny asked as she picked up the final piece of bread.

"I couldn't even tell Mark that I wanted a glass of water without freezing up," I joked. "What do you think?"

"Oh, great!" she said. "Remind me to go to the bathroom to check my reflection in five minutes to make sure I've not got half a garlic plant still in my mouth."

"Garlic grows on plants?"

"I have absolutely no idea," she said, and smiled a perfectly garlic less grin.

Shortly after we'd finished the garlic bread Mark arrived with our main courses, and I still couldn't figure out what was Classic about Jenny's Lasagne. Eating whilst holding a conversation is somewhat of a struggle, but we ate and talked without doing too much of the other. Whilst eating we chatted about school and family and Jenny's council meetings, and Dana and Derek. I was constantly finding out more about her, she was an only child, she told me her parents were both lawyers and they travelled a lot for work. Jenny was left alone in her house most of the time, she told me how she gets lonely in the house so she busies herself with as many extracurriculars as she could just for a reason to be out of the house.

We gossiped a bit and she asked if Derek had told me anything about Dana, which he hadn't. Jenny said she thought they'd been getting closer and closer recently, and that she'd love it if they got together so that we could all double-date. Personally, I hadn't noticed anything going on, but I have a habit of being pretty oblivious to that type of stuff.

By this point in the conversation, we'd both finished our meals. Mark cleared our plates and told us he'd come back in a few minutes for our dessert order. I did a mental calculation in my head and worked out if I had enough money for dessert. I did.

"So…" Jenny began. "What is… this?"

"A very American version of an Italian restaurant," I joked, but this time she didn't laugh. We were getting to the serious part of the evening. "Right… You're the confused one, you tell me."

"Well this evening's been so lovely and you've been so lovely and you've made me forget about all the bad things."

"Is there a but? I'm sensing there's going to be a but."

"There's always a but."

"Always?"

"Most of the time…" she said. "So yeah it's been amazing but there's still so many other factors to consider."

"I disagree, but go on."

"What do you mean you disagree?"

"Well I think if there is a way for you to be happy in life then you should do it, ignore all the doubts and buts and what ifs, and just do what needs doing to make you happy. You can't go your whole life restricting what decisions you make, over thinking everything and eventually not doing something that will make you happy. Because five or ten years down the line, you'll look back and you'll regret not making the decision that would make you happy. What decision would make you happy?"

"Being with you makes me happy."

14

"So…" Jenny said. "What now?"

"Well, I guess that's kind of up to you," I replied. "I mean, we both know what we want, and I'm fairly sure what we want is the same thing. So I'd assume the next logical step is to, you know, go for it."

"Go for it? That's your master plan?"

It was hardly a plan of great detail, but being with Jenny was what, and all, I wanted. She made me happy in a way that no one else could. But more than that she made me feel whole, complete and entirely visible for the first time in my life.

There were times growing up when I knew Jenny was who I wanted. I'd been with her all through her childhood, she just didn't really notice. I was there in fifth grade when she wanted to be President of the United States. She cried when she failed a spelling test because she was sure they wouldn't let her be President if she couldn't spell. Even though I wanted to, I didn't tell her that there five Presidents of the United States were dyslexic and probably couldn't spell (Jefferson,

Wilson, Washington, Jackson, and most famously, JFK).

In seventh grade, she broke her arm filling in for a cheerleader who was ill. She had no idea how to do any of the routines but she just wanted to help her friends. Most of the people in our class signed her cast, but she didn't ask me to do it, and I sure as hell wasn't going to go up to her and ask if I could.

I was there when she was elected student president in eleventh grade, hell, I even voted for her. Not that I cared what she would bring to the role, or what her manifest contained. I voted for her because I knew how much she wanted it, and I wanted to contribute in some way to making her happy.

Now I had another chance to make her happy, and that was exactly what I was going to do.

"That's my plan and I'm sticking to it," I said.

"Hmmm… and what else does this plan involve?"

"Well for one I was thinking more of this," I said, gesturing to our surroundings. "Dates in not-so-Italian Italian restaurants, or wherever else you want. Maybe somewhere less garlicky so we can, two, kiss a lot because that was a hell of a lot of fun, if you ask me."

"I see," she said. "Is there a three?"

"You tell me."

"We don't have to speak in rhymes the whole time, do we?" she said. I snorted a laugh and then she added, "that one was totally unintentional I swear!"

"I'm not sure I believe that."

"There… that's my condition three. Complete trust, honesty, truth, yada yada. Finding out Jordan kept so much from me, it's... well, it's not nice. Just don't keep anything from me."

"Of course I won't," I promised, and she smiled. Outside, a car drove past and its headlights illuminated our table. Jenny's eyes shone under the light and her necklace sparkled. "So... about that kissing thing?" I joked, at that point, Mark came over to kiss-block me and asked if we would like desserts. We hadn't looked but I got the feeling that neither of us wanted to keep Mark waiting any longer.

"Two of whatever's good?" I asked both Jenny and Mark. Our waiter looked to Jenny for an approving nod before scribbling something down on his notepad and scurrying off with a "Right you are then, be back shortly with something good."

Mark didn't disappoint. He came back minutes later with what can only be described as chocolatey heaven with ice cream, it was the first bit of food we'd had that didn't taste Italian, even if the restaurant did such a poor job in pretending to be one. It was a cheesecake sponge ensemble that was entirely un-Italian in every detail right down to the obviously American chocolate chips. And I say obviously American because the best contribution America has made to the dessert industry is realising that everything tastes better with chocolate chips. From cookies to donuts to ice cream, there is no dessert that isn't bettered by the addition of small pieces of chocolate. True fact.

After our dessert plates were empty and our stomachs were full, we had another completely hilarious conversation about nothing in particular until Mark came over with our cheque. This part of the date is, supposedly, a massive indicator into the future of the relationship. Who leans for the cheque first, who pays what and who doesn't, but for us it wasn't a big deal at all. The entire bill meal came to $52.95 – Italian food at American prices, clearly. It was steep but Dad had worked out how much I would need pretty much perfectly. He must be more knowledgeable in teen dating than I first realised. Who knew? I dropped the three twenty dollar notes on the tray and stood up.

"Shall we get out of here?"

"Sounds good," Jenny said, and we both stood up. As we walked out we waved goodbye and shouted our thanks to Mark. We left the restaurant and Jenny's hand found mine as we walked around the back of the restaurant towards the car park.

"Thanks for that, Alex," Jenny said. "I had a really good time. Like, really good!"

I smiled and gripped her hand tighter to tell her that I did too. "I kind of don't want to go home yet, do you?" she said, and I said no. "Let's just drive around for a bit so the night doesn't have to end yet."

Together, as two insignificant dots in a small patch of the earth, we drove around for hours that felt like minutes, and all of my decisions and all of their consequences had led to that girl. This was the start of our relationship, we would later agree that if we were to have an 'anniversary' it would be that day. January the 7th.

February

15

Being one half of the most prestigious couple in school didn't come without difficulties. For example: every boy wanted what I had. I was sure of that because a few months ago I was one of the boys wanting what Jordan had.

I was determined not to ruin it. I don't understand how Jordan could have messed it up. How could he have taken her for granted the way he did? How could anyone cheat on Jenny Evans? The girl defines beauty. I don't know what Jenny finds attractive in me, but I'm happy there's something. I tried to quell the part of my subconscious that told me she was only with me because I saved her life.

Even though she seemed happy with me, I couldn't help feeling that I needed to impress her. Since we'd been together I'd had the overwhelming feeling that I wasn't good enough for her. The only impressive thing I've done is save her life. In my spare time, or when bored in classes, I let my mind wander, and began picturing new ways I could save her. I wasn't planning on throwing her in front of a bus, just to jump in and save her again, but I felt that if I didn't start living up to my self-made reputation, her interest would fade.

I started having these thoughts around the time that Jordan found out that we were together. He found me alone in the hallways between classes. He wasn't alone, he had Fists Three, Five and Six with him.

"She must have hit her head pretty bad when you pushed her over if she's ended up with you...." he said, and I realised he was talking about the bus. "Seriously, how could she have gone from me to you? That's like crashing a Ferrari and buying a Ford to replace it. It's like losing an iPhone and replacing it with a fax machine… it's like…" he paused.

"Like winning the Super Bowl one year, and then not even making the playoffs the next year!" Fist Three continued.

"At least Jordan's insults were imaginative," I spat at Fist Three. I'd had enough of Jordan and his friends and everything to do with him. "Seriously, my brother could come up with a better insult than that, and he's a deaf 13-year-old." I turned to face Jordan, and looked him in the eyes. "If you have nothing else to say, I'll be going now." I wasn't afraid of Jordan any more, I used to bite my tongue and hold back my retorts if he ever got on my case, but he couldn't hurt me anymore, not now that everyone knew about it. I wasn't going to let him ruin my life any more, not now I had something worth fighting for.

"As long as you're okay with being Jenny's rebound, Morgan. Because that's all you are to her, I was with her for years, I know her. She's using you to get back at me. But that's the thing, for me this is funny, watching you fall for her and convince yourself that she loves you when you and I both know she doesn't. She's only with you because you saved her life and she feels sorry for you. Or you can keep pretending and it'll only hurt more when she dumps you, either way is fine for me. She's gonna come crawling back to me when she's done with you, but I won't have her back, the slut." Jordan was angrier than I'd ever seen him. He didn't ever really seem pissed off or mad when he would beat me up, he did it for pleasure. Sick fuck. This was different. This was proper rage. But I was angry too.

"If she's such a slut then why did you skank off to Stacey for a bit on the side? Jenny not enough for you?"

"Actually, not that it is any of your business or anything, but Jenny never put out with me, so I had to get some action from somewhere. So yeah you're right, I guess Jen isn't a slut, she's a frigid bitch."

I'd never asked and never known explicitly that they had, but I always just assumed that Jenny and Jordan had slept together, I guess I was wrong. It took me back slightly, and Jordan clearly noticed.

"What's the matter? You put off her now you know she's not gonna put out any time soon? That's why I got out when I could. Moved on to Stacey where services are... easier. If you get what I mean." He nudged Fist 3 and winked at him.

"You're such an ass," I said, and I turned around and walked out of his sight.

Jordan is an ass, I knew that, and he was just saying whatever he could to get under my skin. But the problem is that it worked. The doubt of not being good enough was already planted inside my head and then Jordan had come along with a fresh batch of fertilizer, some water and a crap tonne of sunlight and the seed of an idea was suddenly growing into something more. I was beginning to have real doubts.

I tried to convince myself that we were happy. We saw each other a hell of a lot, we met up between the classes we don't share, and sit together in the classes we do. We ate lunch together every day, along with Dana and Derek. The Cheerfollowers ate on a separate table, to my delight, and their anger.

Derek and Dana are getting along well, he loved the new lifestyle as much as me, and even though she's 'boring', in his words, he seems to like Dana, and it doesn't seem completely unrequited. He eventually confided in me that the reason he'd ended up in that upstairs room on the night I kissed Jenny for the first time was because that night he and Dana found their way to an empty room and kissed as well. They'd found each other when they realised Jenny and I were nowhere to be seen, continued drinking and eventually ended up alone together. Later, Derek looked out of the window and saw Jenny and me replicating what he and Dana had just done.

Neither of them had brought it up since he told me, so Jenny and I decided not to either. He'd miss this as much as I would, so I knew I'd have to bring him in to help if things started going downhill. One night during a pretty lively Quake game I told him what Jordan had said to me.

"To be honest mate, I'm surprised you've lasted this long," he said. "I thought she'd take one look at your pencil dick and never be able to look you in the eye again due to – watch your left – chronic hysteria."

"We haven't – fuck, get behind – had sex, you know that. Nor did she have sex with Jordan, I've just found out."

"Wow, who knew? – watch this, BANG BANG BANG" he said, as he took out three enemies with three bullets.

"I see in your new found popularity you haven't forgotten how to play Quake."

"Yeah man, unlike you I haven't forgotten where I belong. I know I'm out of my depth and that it won't be long till you and I are back here on Saturday nights, instead of at Mason's." Derek took out two more enemies; I got one of them as they respawned.

"What makes you say that? – SHIT" I asked, as I got shot in the face with a ray gun, Derek quickly avenged my death.

"Jenny loves drama mate. She's gone from being with the star footballer who cheated on her, to some skinny kid who saved her life. You're gonna have to keep her entertained somehow, if you're still not pricking her with your dickstick." Derek really did have a way with words.

"I'd been thinking the same thing actually, just in a less vulgar way – I'll go left you go right," I said, taking control of the conversation and our strategy in the game. "This sounds crazy, but what Jordan said made me think that maybe she's got a bit of a hero complex. He made her sound like she's some kind of damsel in distress who always needs saving, and I was there to save her, and that's the only reason she wants me."

"You poor bastard, a beautiful girl wants you."

"You know what I mean, though?" A grunt from Derek encouraged me to continue. "I think I'm going to have to keep up this hero thing if I'm going to have any chance of keeping her."

"What's your plan?"

"Go up the stairs and flank them – I really don't know man. Any ideas?"

"Fake a mugging, rescue her cat from a tree, save her from a burning building. I don't fucking know," Derek suggested.

"She doesn't have a cat," I said.

"'Shame. That would be your only chance to see her pussy," Derek joked. I threw a virtual grenade at him as payback for that remark, but he turned his character around, caught it and threw it right back at me. It exploded in my face. The "NO LIVES REMAINING" message flashed up on my half of the screen.

Derek's voice taunted me.

"You'll have to try harder than that."

16

Apart from the parental advice they'd each given me before the meal at Le Italiano, my Mum and Dad had stayed relatively quiet about what was happening with Jenny. To be fair, it was new to all of us. But one morning before school Mom told me that she'd like me to invite Jenny round our house for dinner.

"It would be nice to get to know her properly," she'd said. I was fine with that, it was more the 'her getting to know them' bit that I had a problem with.

I brought this up with Jenny during lunch later that day.

"So, what do you think? You up for it?" I asked.

"Uhmm, yeah sure. What day do you want me to come over? I can't do Thursday because me and Dana are going to the grand opening of that new boutique down by the bowling alley. And on Wednesday I have a student council meeting." A part of my brain way in the back had a thought that she was trying to find a way out of it. "I might be able to do Friday though, how is Friday for you?"

"Friday is perfect," I said, kissing her. "As are you."

She giggled and kissed me back, the warmth radiating off her skin told me she was blushing. I was being stupid, she does like me.

"Excuse me, lovebirds." Derek's voice roused us from our embrace. I was so caught up in Jenny, I'd completely forgotten there were other people at the lunch table. "These meatballs tasted like shit on the way down, and I'm sure they'll taste just as bad on the way up if you continue to make me feel like barfing."

I was about to make some witty comeback, but Jenny beat me to it.

"You're just jealous you don't have anyone to make out with at lunch," she said. And then she very deliberately looked from Derek to Dana and back again. This action did not go unnoticed by either of them. They both went a deep shade of crimson and stuttered without actually saying anything, doing their best to avoid eye contact with anyone, especially each other. I looked at Jenny and smiled. "Perfect," I repeated, and she leaned in to kiss me again. Any doubts I felt about her a few days ago had vanished. For a while, at least.

I struggled through the week and met Jenny at her car after last period on Friday. Although I got my license as soon as I turned 16, I'd never gotten around to buying a car, Mom and Dad never offered to buy me one, and I sure as hell wasn't going to ask. In the very unusual case that I needed to use a car, Mom would let me borrow hers. My masculinity is threatened slightly by the fact my girlfriend drives me everywhere, but then again, I was never that masculine in the first place.

We drove to her house so she could get changed before dinner with my parents. On the drive I reached over and grabbed her right hand, she protested "I need both my hands to drive!" but gripped my hand tightly anyway.

We arrived at her empty house. As usual, her parents were out of town. It wasn't the first time I'd been to Jenny's house, but it was the first time I'd been there sober. Jenny has 'small get-togethers' whenever her parents are away on business. These 'get-togethers' usually turn into raging house parties, which end with me and Jenny asleep in her bed.

The first time I saw Jenny's bedroom was the weekend after January 7th. As usual, Jenny's parents were on a business trip so Jenny had a few people over. And by a few, I mean a few dozen. That's kind of how house parties work in this town: you invite one person and you expect them to bring six to ten others with them. Jenny invited me, I brought Derek, who brought Mason, who brought Meowth, who brought Sahira (the girl Dana was tutoring in the library, who it turns out is Meowth's girlfriend) and they brought 2 people from their own crowds. It's a sort of a domino effect of invites.

The party ended up getting pretty out of control, as they often do. But as long as it doesn't get too out of control that it becomes un-clean-up-able for the next day, then it was a pretty successful party. And this one was exactly that. It was a bring your own booze type of thing, people turned up with crates of beer and high alcohol percentage spirits and shot glasses. The deal was that no one was allowed to leave until all the drink was gone, and that's what happened. I spent most of the evening with Meowth, Sahira and Derek as Jenny flitted around the house playing hostess. Meowth came to most parties, and he was always a laugh. He took his new nickname in great spirits; he said that having a nickname made him feel very American.

Am I not officially American until I get a nickname? I wondered. Mason called me AJ once, after Alexander James, but I didn't like that. AJ sounds very Saved By The Bell.

To be honest, every time someone calls Meowth by his nickname I swell with a somewhat unfounded sense of pride. Because I started that. People have followed after something that I said. It was new. It was nice.

I had adapted to this new lifestyle pretty quickly, so by this point I felt pretty comfortable at these parties. It seemed so long ago that a Saturday night at Jenny's house party would've seemed like a pipedream. But now it was real, and I was there and I was drunk. We all were. We were forgetting about everything that didn't involve drinking, dancing, or each other. The music got louder and so did the conversations, the dancing got sillier and so did the drinking games. It was messy but the cardinal rule was abided by. Nothing was broken beyond repair and her house was not beyond clean-up.

Because we knew we had to finish all the drink, there was no chance any of us were going to be driving home. So when the party quietened down at about 4am everyone found somewhere to sleep, Dana asked permission from Jenny to sleep in her parent's bedroom, to which Jenny agreed. I can only assume that Derek followed her in there, but I never asked him. Meowth and Sahira slept on the couch. Jenny did a final check-up around the house, she made sure everyone was settled down with somewhere to sleep, and then she grabbed my hand and we walked to her room.

—

We pulled up to her house and went inside, only now did I begin to notice the things I never noticed whilst intoxicated. Her house is huge, that much I could tell at any time, but it wasn't its size that made it feel so big. It feels empty, which adds to its vastness. There's minimal furniture, hardly any ornaments or pictures, nothing that makes it feel warm or welcoming.

I guess, with her parents working away a lot, they never felt the need to make it feel homely, it's just somewhere to crash between business trips. Despite its size and extravagance, there are things missing from Jenny's house that make my home feel like a home. There are no scuff marks on the walls as a result of running around playing games as a kid, there are no wilted flowers that no one has gotten around to replacing. In my house, we have a door frame with dozens of pencil marks on it, from where my Dad measured our height as we grew up. He would write the date next to each pencil mark, so we'd know next time how much we'd grown since last time. In my house the couch has each of our individual ass prints on it, the couch here doesn't look like it's ever been used. It's merely there because it should be there, as an existential and essential piece of the suburban family jigsaw. Meowth and Sahira sleeping on it was probably the most action the poor thing had seen in months.

It made me sad, seeing the house in a new light, so I put my arm around Jenny. She must have been thinking the same thing because she said: "It looks different during the day, doesn't it?"

I didn't know what to say, so I just nodded and followed her upstairs. Her bedroom is the only part of the house that feels lived in, it's more personalised than the entire rest of the house is. Posters of boy bands, classmates, cheerleaders, and sports teams peeling off the walls. No inch of wallpaper was visible behind the posters. It was kind of intimidating being in a room full of shirtless Zac Efrons.

Stuck to the ceiling above her bed are a bunch of glow in the dark dolphin stickers. I asked her about them the first time we slept in the room together.

"As a kid, I was scared of the dark," she said. "My Dad put them there and told me they'd keep me safe. Dolphins were my favourite animal. I guess my Dad never got around to taking them down, and I'm not tall enough to reach them."

I sensed this was a lie. If she wanted to take them down she could've just stood on a chair, or reached them with a ruler. I think she wants to keep them there as a memoir to her childhood. I don't mention this to her though, not wanting to intrude on her nostalgia. I'd spent too long looking at things in her room, when I snapped out of it she was stood smiling at me, wearing nothing but a tank top and her underwear.

"I cannot believe that you're staring at a school of fluorescent dolphins when I'm stood right here in my underwear," she said with a wry smile.

"The collective term for dolphins is 'pod', actually," I corrected.

"You are such a nerd," she said and took a few steps closer to me. She erased the distance between us quickly. When she reached me she pushed me back onto the bed and sat on top of me. "But I wouldn't have you any other way."

17

It's a 15 minute drive from Jenny's house to mine, traffic dependent. That gave me far too long to dwell on what had just happened. My streak of firsts was continuing: first time in Jenny's house whilst sober, first time seeing Jenny in her underwear, first base, second base, third. I don't know whether she stopped it or I stopped it, but it stopped. And all I could think to say as she stared across the bed into my eyes was "We should probably get dressed, Mom will hit the roof if we're late."

Then she either smiled a sigh or sighed a smile – I wasn't quite sure – and rose silently to put her clothes on. I did the same, and minutes later we were in the car. We said very little in the car ride. It wasn't an awkward silence, it never was between us, but there was a noticeable tension. A new barrier had been crossed, and it had triggered this air of uncertainty. I couldn't help but feel that I may have disappointed her.

She pulled into the driveway behind my Mom's Toyota, and got out of the car. "I love you," I whispered after the door had closed behind her. I got out too, joined her on the porch step, grasped her hand tight, squeezed and then let go.

"Here goes nothing," I said, and she chuckled. I could tell we were both nervous.

I had an urge to reach out and knock at the door, but then I remembered that it's my house, and my girlfriend standing next to me. With a sudden air of confidence, I opened the door and went in.

"MOM!" I shouted. "I'M HOME, JENNY'S HERE TOO." I knew she'd be upstairs applying and reapplying her makeup. I knew Dad would be sat in the front room in front of the television, watching it but not taking anything in. I knew Charlie would be in his room, reading probably. "I'LL BE DOWN IN A MINUTE, I'M DOING MY FACE. GO SIT WITH YOUR FATHER," Mom shouted from upstairs, Jenny followed me into the front room, where I realised I got one of my predictions wrong. Charlie was sat watching TV with Dad. Two out of three ain't bad, I guess.

"Dad, Jenny. Jenny, Dad." I gestured from one to the other then back again.

"Nice to see you again, Mr Morgan," said Jenny.

"The pleasures all mine, and please, call me Dave," said Dave. Charlie arrived at my side, and looked up at me, expectantly.

"Charlie, you remember Jenny," I signed to him. "Just wave," I spoke aloud to Jenny.

"Actually, I asked Derek to teach me some sign language earlier. How's this?" said Jenny. I was speechless. Incredible.

"I have large cans," Jenny signed to Charlie. Charlie and I erupted into laughter, even my Dad let out an amused snort. I guess that was Derek's payback for her comment about him and Dana earlier in the week. If it wasn't so hysterical, I'd be pissed at him. I made a mental note to congratulate him the next time I saw him.

"What's so funny?" Jenny asked me out loud.

My Dad answered before I could. "You just told Charlie you have large breasts," he said and walked out of the room laughing. My Dad wasn't a laugher, he rarely found things funny, nor did my Mom. It was good to hear laughter in the house for once.

Jenny's face went scarlet. For a moment I thought she'd storm out of the house. But to her credit, she didn't. Charlie tapped her on the arm to get her attention, then gave her a sign that even Jenny would've understood. The universal sign for **'Thank you'**. An extended palm touching his mouth, he moved his hand away from lips. It almost looked like he was blowing her a kiss. He followed Dad out of the room, leaving Jenny and me alone.

"I only told him I had big boobs. Why is he thanking me?"

I knew the answer right away. "Because you tried."

She blushed again, this time for a positive reason, dark pink skin contrasting with her bright blonde hair.

The sound of Mom's footsteps as she came down the stairs was our cue to follow the rest of my family, into the dining room. "Here goes nothing," she whispered to me

Dinner went as smoothly as I could have hoped. My Mom can be a pretty tough character to handle sometimes, but Jenny did a stellar job. Even though it should've been Mom asking Jenny questions in a bid to get to know her better, my Mom has never been one to sit in silence, so most of it was just Mom talking at Jenny and Jenny listening.

Mom cooked pot roast and was delighted that Jenny wasn't 'one of those vegetarian types' and even more delighted that Jenny managed to finish most of her decently sized portion, exclaiming 'There's nothing wrong with a bit of meat on the bones,' and, 'Thank the lord for gravy, am I right girl?' This was weird for two reasons, 1) I'd never heard my Mom call anyone 'girl' and 2) Mom isn't a religious person at all — us kids aren't either. Dad is, but he's quiet about it. Then again, he's quiet about most things.

As the meal finished, Jenny offered to help clear away and wash up, Mom declined her offer by saying "Leave it to the boys, you and I can go have a girly chat!" Jenny looked at me, pleadingly, so I nodded to Charlie, encouraging him to go with them for moral support. "So, what'd you think?" I asked Dad, amidst the soapy water bubbles.

"She's nice," Dad said, as blunt as ever. "But you should just go careful, Alex."

"What'd you mean?" I asked, slightly taken aback.

"Just go careful."

18

Just go careful. I repeated to myself what my Dad had said to me. I tried to ask him what he meant by it, but Charlie came bursting in with a desperate look on his face that told me that Jenny needed help dealing with Mom. He has this unnatural gift of following conversations, even though he can't hear what's being said. He follows body language, the way people sit in their seats, fidget when they're getting uncomfortable. It's incredible how he does it. That's how he would've known that Jenny was struggling to cope with Mom by herself.

I never got the chance to go back and talk to my Dad, which just left me to wonder what he meant. Maybe he meant that I was falling too hard too fast, but I doubted that. He's a great believer in true love, that's why he's stayed with my Mom all these years, even though she is how she is. Maybe he had sensed that things had taken a further step between us, physically, an hour earlier. But how could have known that? Was he telling me to slow down? Giving me some fatherly advice? Was that his way of having 'the talk' with me?

Since the second my Dad said it, I'd been panicking. What if I lose her? What if I lose everything? I asked myself repeatedly. I couldn't lose this now, not after having everything. I couldn't go back to how things were before this. Before Jenny. I'd do anything to keep her.

I pondered on this for the weekend, a weekend I spent alone. There was no party on Saturday night, or if there was, I wasn't invited to it. Jenny was busy with Dana, I can't remember what they were doing. Derek was on a fishing trip with his Dad. So I spent the weekend alone in my room, whilst the earth rotated and I stayed still, wondering. I thought by now it was too late to go and ask Dad himself, he would have forgotten what he meant, caught up in the moment or something like that.

It wasn't until Monday morning that I was able to voice my concerns to Derek. I asked him what he thought my Dad meant, and he took significantly less time thinking about an answer than I had.

"Well it's obvious really, isn't it?"

"It is?"

"Well yeah, it's obvious to all of us mate. She's too good for you," he said. "You walked into that house with someone that looks like she's fallen straight out of a Victoria's Secret catalogue, your Dad takes one look at her and could see straight up that something wasn't right." Derek spoke a lot more metaphorically recently, I'd noticed.

"You think?"

"Yeah of course, 'just go careful' is a warning that sooner or later, you're going to get dumped and the more into this girl you get, the harder it's going to hurt when she drops your ass. It's like that quote from that girl in that book we read in English class. "When you're floating up and up in your bubble, the higher you climb, the further you have to fall.""

"Oh," was all I could say. There was a short silence as Richardson walked into the room, so I signed to Derek "we need to start planning."

"Later," he replied and if hands could convey emotions, his would be excited.

Since first talking about it with Derek I'd given the hero complex thing a lot of thought, and I'd come up with my first plan.

Even though he had said it in jest, Derek's 'fake a mugging' idea resonated with me somehow. That would be my next way of impressing Jenny; I would fake a mugging.

Derek would help me, I'm sure of it. I know this is all in my head, I'm being crazy, she probably does like me for me, and not just because I saved her life. And even if that's the reason she started to like me, after the amount of time we've spent together, she must have developed some feelings for me, right? I try to convince myself that I'm being stupid, but it can't hurt to have a backup plan.

It turned out impossible to talk at all during the school day. We tried to sneak off for a discussion during lunch, but Jenny beckoned me over to the table she was sat on. I sat down next to her and she didn't plant a kiss on my cheek, like she normally does.

She seemed off, but I didn't have the courage to ask what was wrong. I had my own shit to deal with.

All through lunch she seemed weird with me, which only meant that this plan needed forming, and performing, soon.

Derek beat me home. He was sat on my front porch playing a game on his phone when I got back.

"Nice of you to join me," he said without looking up from his game.

"I did text you to let you know to come over a bit later."

"Wouldn't't've seen it. Been stuck on this level since 4th period."

"Glad to know you're taking your education seriously," I said, opening the door. "You coming in?"

"You make me wait half an hour outside in the cold, and now you can't wait one stinking minute for me to finish this level?"

I peered down at his phone, and recognised the game. "I'll be grey-haired by the time you've finished then. You can only complete that level if you buy the booster pack from the in-game store," I said, knowing full well Derek would never spend money on a cell phone game.

"You could've told me that a few hours ago. God knows what I missed in 5th period Poly-Sci."

"Not even God could help you pass Poly-Sci. I still don't know why you took it." But I did know, Dana took that class as well, he sits behind her. He denies it, but even though he always classified her as the boring one, he's always had a thing for her. "You coming in or what? You're letting the heat out."

"Yeah yeah, keep your knickers on Shirley," he said, following me inside. "Let's get planning"

March

19

Together, we formulated a plan. I would make up some reason to take Jenny to the mall, I ignored Derek's suggestion of "There's a sale on edible underwear." Derek would also be at the mall, wearing a dark jacket with the hood up over his head. He would run up to Jenny, grab her bag and run off. We figured the best place for a fake mugging is somewhere out of the way.

If someone saw this happen, Derek could actually get arrested – pretty much fucking up the plan. So we agreed we'd do it as Jenny came out of the restroom. We'd decided on a restroom on the third floor, because there was a long corridor from the restrooms back into the main shopping area. That way I could chase Derek down the corridor, sprint around the corner out of sight, and get Jenny's bag back before she got to him. It would make me look like the hero I thought she needed me to be. Or maybe, the hero I needed myself to be.

Getting Jenny to the mall was easy enough, I told her at lunch that I wanted to pick up some things for

Charlie's birthday, and that there was a really cool gadget store which sold things I know he'd like. When we got to the mall we browsed around the first two floors for a while. I made sure to buy a large soda for us to share.

I was taking my time, waiting for the diet Mountain Dew to do take its toll on her bladder. But at no point did she say she needed the toilet, so on the way out of Gadgets Gadgets Gadgets, I had to improvise.

"I really need the toilet, you coming?" I asked, not at all subtle.

"Um, no. I'm good thanks. I'll wait here, there's a restroom down that hallway," she said, pointing at the hallway next to the gadget shop, at the end of which, Derek was waiting in a cubicle in a black jacket. Waiting for me.

"You sure?" I asked. "We might not be home for a bit. I need to get some more stuff."

"I'm honestly fine, besides, public bathrooms freak me out."

"Uh okay. Be back in a bit then," I said, and kissed her on the cheek.

I walked down the corridor, looking behind me to check she was still stood at the end. I racked my brain trying to think of what do next. It's too risky to fake the mugging out in the main plaza of the mall, there are people around. They'd come to help, surely, won't they?

I opened the door to the male toilets and knocked on the far cubicle three times, as instructed. I thought the secret knock was a ridiculous idea, but Derek insisted. "Is she in there? Is it go time? What took so long? Are you ready?" he asked without stopping for any answers.

"We have a problem," I said. "She's adamant she doesn't need a piss, so she's waiting for me at the end of the corridor."

"Oh, that's not too bad. I say we still go ahead with the plan, it'll be more exciting this way anyway, make you look like an even bigger hero. What do you say to that, double-oh-three-and-a-half?" he said, and gestured to my crotch.

"You're the one that will end up in jail, so why not."

"Yeah, but it's the mall jail, it's where they take the toddlers that have lost their parents in Selfridges. It's hardly full of rapists and murderers," he said, holding the door open for me.

"It's your ass," I said, and walked through the door and headed back to Jenny. Derek hung back a minute.

"You took a while," she said as I got back.

"Oh, yeah, there was, uh, a line for the cubicle, I said. I looked back down the corridor and saw Derek walking towards us. Showtime.

"Come on, I need to get a card," I said, taking Jenny's hand and leading her away from the restroom. And at that moment Derek struck. He ran full pelt at Jenny, hood down to cover his face and swiped for her bag. She didn't see it coming at all. Her clutch bag was ripped from her arms and Derek ran. Even though I knew it was going to happen, it still took me a second to react. Jenny's scream prompted me into action and I took flight.

Immediately, I noticed a flaw in our plan: we hadn't discussed how I would actually take the bag off of him without revealing his identity. I decided on an equally realistic and dramatic approach would be to tackle him to the ground. After a short chase, I lunged at him and caught him by the waist, hurtling us both onto the floor. He dropped the bag behind us, and as I stood up to grab it he dashed in the other direction. A perfect execution. Almost.

As I stood up, bag in hand and began to walk back to Jenny, I saw just about the last person I wanted to see, and the second, third, fourth, fifth, and sixth last persons I wanted to see. Jordan and Gang Member's Two, Three, Four, Five and Six. They were all staring at me, their mouths ajar. They were stood next to Jenny, who wore an expression of shock and awe.

"That was some tackle, Morgan," said one of the indistinguishable numbers, as I approached them. "True enough," said another, Daniel, I think.

"Impressive," said Jordan, but his voice didn't sound impressed. I handed Jenny's bag back to her, her face still in shock, grabbed her by the hand and pulled her away.

I wondered why they were there. What kind of cosmological blip in the timeline of my existence made it so that at the exact moment in time I had just engineered the mugging of my girlfriend, her ex-boyfriend shows up and sees the whole thing.

"Are you okay?" she asked after a long silence.

"I'm fine. How are you? Did he hurt you at all?"

"I'm fine," she said. "Thank God you were here."

20

It was messy, it didn't go exactly as planned, but it was successful. Jenny's 'mugging' had shocked her, and she was more grateful than ever to have me around to save her. The whole situation was so successful that it earned me a drunken toast at Mason's next party. Or they thought they knew, at least.

"To Alex, for saving our Jenny's perfect little ass once again," Mason said, raising his plastic cup of beer into the air. Other cups joined his and pointed towards to the ceiling, knocking into one another, beer sloshed over the tops of over-filled cups, and they said my name in chorus. "To Alex."

The feeling I had that night was why I did it. The mugging. People cheered my name, slapped me on the back. Appreciated me. People looked at me, instead of through me. Passed me drinks instead of passing me in the hallways. Everything was better. I was happier than I had ever been. I had everything I wanted. I thought I might regret it, but how could I when it made me feel that good? At a rager surrounded by people that I could call my friends. That would be unthinkable at the start of the year. Unfathomable. Everything was gold. Golden. Drunk. And I got to keep my best friend. He's here with me. Fitting in. Drunk.

I looked towards Derek. He was sat on the counter between two of Jenny's Cheerfollowers – both blond, both as drunk as him, both with a hand on his leg. He'd somehow convinced people he'd had a part to play in Jenny's saviour.

"Taught him everything he knows, didn't I? How else do you think a skinny guy like him could've tackled a mugger that size?" I heard him telling the Cheerfollowers. Complimenting yourself in a fake story about a fake mugging? Nice Derek, nice. He was enjoying himself. I began to scan the rest of the kitchen. Standing in the doorway I saw Dana, her eyes were trained directly on Derek and the blondes. What looked like a tear formed in her eye as she noticed me looking. She turned and walked straight out of the kitchen. I followed her, ignoring the shouts of "Alexxxxxxx you're wasted," from an increasingly drunk Mason. I'd already lost sight of Dana by the time I left the kitchen, but I followed in the direction I thought she was headed – towards more alcohol.

I pass by my equals, my peers, seniors, juniors. Most people acknowledged me – the ones that didn't were too busy drinking, or kissing, or smoking to notice me. My drink is filled before it's empty. My quest to find Dana was stop-start because I got stopped by various people at the party who start conversations with me. Then Daniel Marks stops me. And starts.

I didn't realise he was at the party, but it made sense. He was friends with Mason a long time before I was. "Hey," he said, his eyes were foggy enough that I could tell he was drunk, or worse.

"Hey," I said.

"I haven't forgotten, you know. I never have, you know what I'm talking about. I've never said anything, but I haven't forgotten." It took me a few moments to figure out what he was talking about. "You saved me like you saved Jenny. You saved her twice. And look what's happened to you since you saved me. I mean, before all that happened and you got cool or whatever. Before that you were, well I don't know what you were. I didn't know you. But Jordan knew you and he, well, I don't need to tell you what he's like. But I'm sorry Alex. It should've been me where you were. You didn't need to stick up for me like that. But you did. You had my back. You should know that I'll have your back whenever from now on. You know that yeah?"

I doubted that he meant what he said, but it meant a lot that he'd said it. Daniel stumbled off to find a refill of whatever had got him in the state he was in. I turned a corner and found Jenny.

"There you are," she said. "I've been looking for you for an hour."

I wasn't aware that much time had passed, nor did I realise how drunk I was. She walked over and kissed me. And then I was sober, and everything was okay because I belonged there with Jenny's arms around my neck, and mine around her waist, and that is where I will stay. In my happy place. Everything I had done in my life brought me to that moment with Jennifer Anne

Evans. If it meant that I had to take beating after beating from Jordan Wilkes to get to that moment with Jenny, then I could look back on my life and say with hand on heart that every decision I made was the right one, because without each of those decisions I wouldn't have found myself in that moment with the girl that I am in love with.

I was experiencing a natural high from being with Jenny, and probably an artificial one as well – it seemed like they'd hotboxed the entire house, and Mason's house isn't small. Anywhere we walked was through a cloud of smoke. I wondered how long it would take for the smell of weed to leave the house, it was probably permanently embedded into every fabric and cushion and pillow. A mess is clean-up-able. A smell isn't.

Meowth walked past and greeted us with a smile and a wave. He had a drink in each hand, so his wave caused liquid to spill out of each cup. I watched as the perfectly circular droplets of whatever-the-drink-was hit the floor and shattered into hundreds of smaller droplets that did the same thing. I realised there was a metaphor in there somewhere as well, but once again I was too drunk to find it. Derek is better at metaphors than I am. But it reminded me of something. I looked at Jenny.

"Bridge?" I asked.

"I thought you'd never ask," she said. So we went to the bridge above the pond full of metaphors, but it was raining, so we grabbed an umbrella from the umbrella stand and we stood above the bridge and we kissed in the rain and the umbrella did fuck all because we still got wet. There was water above us, below us, on our skin and in our hair and there was a waterfall and it was like drowning, except we were drowning in each other. We ended the night with the dolphins.

April

21

Mom had gotten used to me staying away from home at weekends, I never explicitly told her that I was staying with Jenny most nights, but we'd come to some sort of unspoken agreement not to talk about that type of stuff. She knew that things were different. She knew that my lifestyle had changed, that everything was changing, but she accepted it. She knew that I would always have my phone on me if she needed me urgently, if not, she would expect me home whenever I showed up.

One weekend Jenny suggested we should stay at mine to spend some time with Charlie, so we did exactly that. On Sunday morning the three of us sat down and watched cartoons together, Charlie squished in between Jenny and me on the sofa. Charlie loves watching cartoons, even if he can't hear what's going on. The shapes and the colours and the pace of the action enthral him. We can enable subtitles on our TV, and we even have a special add-on which means on certain programs, there's someone in the corner of the screen signing the words alongside the show. Charlie hardly uses either of these, he prefers to make up the words himself, that way the cartoon runs how he wants it to – it's up to him what happens. I admire his attitude. I think sometimes he forgets that he's deaf. He just carries on with his life and does it his way.

Charlie loves Jenny. She's like a shiny new toy for him to play with. After the cartoons wore him out he fell asleep on her arm. It was a beautiful moment. Charlie isn't normally comfortable with meeting new people – he was so shy around all the doctors in the hospital – but the way he is with Jenny, and the way she is with him is incredible. Considering she is an only child, the almost sibling-like affection Charlie shows her doesn't seem strange to her, it's natural and easy. She strokes his hair as he sleeps.

Dad walked in and took note of the scene, he looked at me and smiled. Am I going careful, Dad? I almost asked him.

BANG. There was a loud crash in the cartoon and Charlie sat up immediately. For a second I stared at him in wonder. I thought that maybe he had heard the noise and it woke him up. But when Jenny apologised for waking him up I realised that the crash on screen must've made Jenny jump, which made Charlie wake up. Even though he couldn't hear her apology, he understood. Jenny's eyes followed him as he stood up and left the room.

Shortly after Charlie got up and left, Jenny did too. She'd been at my house all weekend so she had to go home to get herself ready for school in the morning. We lingered in the hallway a bit as she shouted up the stairs to say goodbye to everyone, and distorted voices shouted back at her. I kissed her goodbye perhaps slightly more passionately than I would've done had my parents been nearer. And then she either smiled a sigh or sighed a smile again before walking out the front door.

From her unwillingness to leave, I got the feeling that she felt more at home with my family than she does at her own house. I felt sorry for her. Our family is dysfunctional but at least we're always there for each other. She has to go home to a big empty house every day and be reminded of the fact that her parents are never there for her anymore.

After she left I felt more alone than I had done in a few days, so I went searching around the house for Charlie. He wasn't in his room or in my room but when I walked into my parent's bedroom I recognised a Charlie sized lump underneath the covers of their bed. Knowing he couldn't hear me coming, I planned to tear the covers off him and scare him.

I tore the covers off the bed. Then I screamed.

Charlie was curled up in a ball with his hands over his ears, his fingers were stained red. I screamed again. A tiny pool of blood formed a circle on my parents' bed sheets. I screamed again.

Footsteps on stairs.

Dad was first to the bedroom, he shot up the stairs like a bat out of hell. He acted quickly, he told me to call an ambulance, he ran to the bathroom, when he returned he started to dab a wet towel at Charlie's ears, trying to clear away some blood to get a better look at what was causing it. Charlie just laid there, eyes open, not daring to move, looking terrified. Mom arrived at my side, grabbed the phone out of my hand and dialled 911. As soon as the operator picked up Mom screamed down the phone and told them to come now, to drop everything and come. From somewhere in the room Dad told me to go get more towels and blankets but I just I stood there. Frozen. Helpless. Mom shouted and Dad talked at Charlie and Charlie was silent and I was silent and I was scared. Six and a half minutes later an ambulance arrived.

22

Two days after the ambulance came, the sound of sirens still rang in my ears. Normally in an emergency, everything moves super fast, but with this, everything stopped. I felt frozen in time and space, I couldn't move, I couldn't help. I was useless. Dad was sensational. He barked orders at everyone, even the paramedics, the doctors weren't in charge; Dad was. Usually, he lets Mom do the talking, he did with my 'accident', but he was so different with Charlie's doctors. He demanded regular updates, but he did it with a tone that Mom could never register, he was forceful yet kind, aggressive yet respectful. And it worked, Charlie got the best treatment possible, everyone loved him, and everyone wanted him to get better. And he did.

I didn't understand much of what the doctor said was wrong with Charlie, my mind wandered as he explained it to us. I looked from Charlie, asleep in his bed, to Jenny, asleep in a chair, to my father, standing eye-to-eye with the doctor, absorbing every word. Much of what the doctor said floated over my head, occasional words and phrases like "auricle bleeding" and "canal inflammation" would stick in my head. I only properly understood what happened when Dad dumbed it down for me later.

"It was basically a residual clot from when they worked on his ears after he lost his hearing. Either someone fucked up his operation before, or something new has developed over time." I had never heard my Dad swear before. "They actually hope that it was someone fucking up before that caused it, because if it's something that's developed over time, they don't know what it is or how to stop it coming back."

"If it's been there all this time, why has this only just happened?" Mom asked the question I had been wondering myself.

"They say it could have been caused by a sudden change in his equilibrium. A sudden movement or something." He looked at Jenny's sleeping figure. He wasn't blaming her out loud, but the subtext was there. He was saying that when she gasped and jumped at the noise from the TV, it tipped some kind of scale inside Charlie's head and burst a clot. I was so glad she was asleep; she didn't need to know that it was her that caused it. It would crush her.

"It doesn't matter who or what caused it," Mom said "Is he going to be okay? Is my baby going to get better?" Mom never called us baby.

"They're confident he will. He didn't lose too much blood, but because it's near his brain they're still a bit concerned." Dad flinched at the word blood, no doubt his brain was filled with flashback images of Charlie led on the bed in a deep red pool of it. I'd been having similar visions, and I was sure my nightmares would be full of the scene too, if I were able to get to sleep, that is. I looked over to Jenny, sleeping on the chair. I wished I could sleep.

My friends arrived at the hospital twenty minutes after we did. As soon as I'd regained my senses and the use of my fingers, I rang Derek to tell him what happened. He said he'd be there with Jenny and Dana within a half hour. Even Mason had offered to come in and visit to make sure we were all okay.

School on Monday was out of the question for me, and Jenny remained adamant that she was going to skip it and stay with me through this. "It's not like my parents are around to reprimand me for skipping school," she had said.

So she stayed with us, Charlie even asked where she had gone one time when he woke up and she wasn't there. **"To get something to drink buddy,"** I signed back to him, and he went back to sleep. I left him with Mom and Dad and went to find her. When I eventually found her she burst into tears on my shoulder.

"I know it's my fault, I heard what your Dad said. I woke up, but I didn't want to intrude, I feel so awful," she said without pausing for breath.

"It's not your fault. The doctors said it was always there, if it wasn't you nudging him on the sofa, it would've been something else, when he was on the swings, or riding his bike. If anything we're lucky it happened when we were all around to help him." I reminded myself that I did nothing to help, I just stood there frozen whilst Dad did everything.

"I guess. But I still feel so awful, your parents must hate me."

"We don't even know if that's what caused it, Jenny. Stop being so hard on yourself."

"I can't help it, Alex."

"Come on, let's just go get some rest. We're all so tense right now."

I dragged her back to Charlie's room, his face lit up as she walked in the room. I'm sure that made it even worse for her because she squeezed my hand tight, sleep deprivation had caught up with me, I suddenly became very aware of how tired I was. I slumped into a chair and crashed.

23

As I feared, my dreams were bright red. I dreamt of nothing coherent, there was no story or plot, it was just an endless reel of blood-stained sheets, fingertips covered in red, and screaming, lots and lots of screaming. I forced my eyes open, turning the dream off – or putting it on standby, at least. Jenny was still next to me; her hand gripped mine as she noticed I had woken up.

"Bad dream?" she asked. "You're sweating."

"No," I lied. "I'm fine. Any news?"

"None that I could understand, go find your Dad. I'll stay here with Charlie."

I got up to leave, kissing Jenny's forehead as I did so, then walked over to a sleeping Charlie and kissed his forehead too. I couldn't find my Dad in the Café or the toilets, I asked a couple of nurses if they knew where he was, none of them did so I carried on looking. I wondered if he had gone home, then dismissed that thought immediately. Eventually, a doctor told me that he was in the doctors' lounge. This struck me as odd; a doctors' lounge is for strictly, well, doctors.

Sure enough, I found him in the doctors' lounge on the third floor, I was told by a grey-haired doctor that I wasn't allowed in, but that he would go hunt down my Dad for me. Dad came out mid-conversation with Charlie's doctor, Dr Perez. I waited until they'd finished and Dr Perez had left before I fired my questions at my Father. "How is Charlie? Where's Mom? Why were you in the doctors' lounge? When can he go home?"

"Better. Home. Research. Today," he answered my questions simply, and like he always had, with as few words as possible.

"Research? What kind of research?"

"I'm just trying to find out everything I can about Charlie's case, I was asking if there are things we can do to make him safer at home."

"You're going to baby proof our home? He's 13 years old. He's fine."

"Clearly not, Alex. Or this wouldn't have happened, would it?"

"Are you fucking serious?" I was suddenly furious, and it took me a while to figure out why. I was jealous. Where was this loving, caring, 'I will do everything I can to protect my child' Dad when I was lying in a hospital bed a few months ago? All Dad did when I was in hospital as far as I saw was just sit there being silent and let Mom do the talking. But now that Charlie was hurt he was suddenly barking orders at paramedics, and talking his way into the doctors' lounge to squeeze any more information out of any doctor he can find.

I hated myself immediately for thinking it, but I couldn't help it. I know that Charlie has been through a lot, so Dad thinks he needs protection, but I've never seen this from him before. Even after the explosion, Dad wasn't like this, Mom was the one that fought with doctors, teachers and anyone that would listen trying to get everything done that Charlie needed doing. Now it was Dad's turn, and Mom was at home? Something wasn't right.

"Why isn't Mom here?" I demanded.

"Your mother is at home making sure that Charlie has a nice clean house to come home to." He didn't say it, but that basically meant 'She had to clean his blood off her sheets.'

Unsatisfied, I turned and left, and Dad didn't call after me or follow me, he just walked back into the doctors' lounge.

I made my way back to Jenny and my brother, she had moved from the chair near the door to the chair by his bedside. I noticed how empty the room looked with just the two of them and all the empty chairs. I thought back to my time in hospital, the room was always packed when I was awake; my family were here, Jenny's family was here, the bus driver was here, journalists came in, my principal came in, heck, even Jordan came in. Now I felt even worse for being jealous of the way Dad was treating Charlie. Charlie has been homeschooled pretty much his whole life, he doesn't have any real friends, none that would come to visit him whilst he was in the hospital anyway. Even before my popularity, before my leg exploded when I got hit by a bus, I still had Derek. Charlie only really has me,

Mom and Dad. I know that Charlie wouldn't be upset that he hadn't had visitors, he wouldn't be jealous that more people came to see me than came to see him. That gave me the strength to forget that my Dad seemingly cares more for Charlie than he does for me.

"Where have you been?" Charlie asked with his hands.

"I went to see Dad to find out when you can go home. He says we can go later today, you just need to wait a bit longer."

"Stay with me," Charlie signed, almost causing me to break down in front of him.

"Of course I will."

24

When Charlie was discharged from hospital the doctors expected us to take him home and pretend that nothing had happened, but it wasn't going to be that easy. Out of all of us, Charlie was the one taking everything the easiest, Dad was worried, Mom was stressed, I was terrified, and Jenny was feeling guilty. But Charlie was none of these things, he just went on living as he always had, with a smile on his face and warmth in his heart. I think part of him even enjoyed his time in the hospital because it brought all of our family together again. I had been AWOL from family life a lot because of my social life, so to him, our family hadn't felt complete for a while, but when he was in hospital we were all there, we were all together. It wasn't that he liked being the centre of attention, I think he just liked that he was able to bring his family together again.

On Wednesday morning Charlie insisted I went back to school, he said that I'd already missed too much because of him. He was probably right, but I still didn't want to leave him. In the end, though he got his way, he always did, not because he was pushy or spoilt, he was just the type of person that you had to please, and you had to do whatever it took to make him happy. And he wanted me to go to school, so that's what I was going to do. Of course, when I got to school, everyone already knew what had happened.

"I heard about your brother man, I hope he's okay." "How's Charlie doing?" "Hope everything's okay Alex." These were the shouts of the faceless crowd as I made my way to first period. I nodded and muttered my appreciation, wishing I could be like Moses and part the sea of high-schoolers that blocked my way to Richardson's class. Jordan was amongst the faces, a smirk on his. Because of the traffic in the halls, I arrived late to Richardson's class, but even Richardson must have heard about Charlie, because he said nothing to me as I walked in late and took my seat.

The one person in the room whose words I cared about gave me a punch on the shoulder. Derek was always there to punch me when I needed it. I turned towards Jenny's desk and she was looking at me, we made eye contact and immediately she turned her head away and hid her face.

I powered through classes until lunch and then skipped the rest of the day, I knew that at lunch I would have more people looking at me apologetically and sympathetically and other types of –etically. I didn't need that.

I text Derek to let him know I wouldn't be at lunch, and that I was going to just walk somewhere and think. He replied "Where are we going?" and met me on my way out of school. His mum had lent him the car, so together we walked towards it, got in, and drove. He didn't ask me anything and I didn't say anything, he knew that I wanted to have my thoughts to myself and that I would talk when I was ready.

I looked out of the window. Spots of rain were already starting to create their own little piece of art on the glass. Beyond the window we drove past houses upon houses, houses that people I know grew up in, houses of people I don't know, houses of people I would never know. We passed an old man walking his dog, he was wearing a dark green raincoat with matching wellies. The dog wore a studded collar with a leash attached, the old man gripped the other end of the leash tightly, making sure the dog couldn't leave him.

We passed a group of women with pushchairs, hoods over their heads and covers on their buggies, keeping the rain off themselves and their children. We passed a homeless man sat by some bins, he had his coat off, relishing the sensation of cold water on his unwashed face. I thought hard about all of these people, about the choices and the mistakes they had made, and about all of the events and circumstances in their lives that brought them to where they were. I thought about the old man, was the dog his only companion? Maybe he was widowed, and the dog was all he had in life to cling to. Maybe he didn't care that it was raining, maybe he didn't care that he was going to get wet and possibly ill because his dog wanted a walk, he was going to do what the dog wanted him to do. Maybe the dog was his only connection to his past memories, to his past experiences.

I thought about the women, gossiping as they rushed home to the warmth, were children part of their plan? Where were the children's fathers? Maybe they were at work earning the money to provide for them all, it was a Wednesday afternoon after all. Maybe the father's had left the mothers to look after the children themselves.

I thought of the homeless man the most, of all the people I had seen in the streets today he looked the happiest. The old man with the dog looked thoughtful, the women with the children looked like they wanted to be anywhere else but where they were, but the homeless man, the one without anywhere to hide from the rain. The one without the dog, or the children as a companion, looked happy. He doesn't have someone whose face lights up when they see him, he has nothing. But he looked genuinely happy. Even though all of the choices he had made in his life had led to the point of him being alone on the streets, even though everyone and everything in his past had gone against him, he was living without a care, genuinely happy because it was raining and he got to experience the infrequent sensation of cold water on his skin.

As it so frequently does, my mind wandered to Jenny. I wondered if she was happy with the choices she had made in life. If she was happy with the path her decision tree had taken. She had something in common with the three subjects of my interest over the past few minutes, she had been left behind; in her case by her parents.

I assumed the man with the dog had been widowed, left by a love that he once cherished. I assumed that the women with the children had been left by their baby daddies, who skipped town because they couldn't deal with the responsibility of a child. I assumed the homeless man had been left by everyone he once held dear.

I assumed these things but I didn't really know they were true. It's possible the man with the dog was on his way to see his beloved wife, that the mothers had loving husbands at home who will greet them with a warm towel and a hot drink, maybe the homeless man has a homeless wife and a homeless child, a family struck down by bad luck. I just have a habit of thinking the worst. I realised then why I'd worked so hard to keep Jenny: because I'm scared of losing people. I was frozen solid as I thought I was going to lose Charlie. I was scared of losing Jenny, scared of losing Charlie, scared that I was going to lose my popularity, lose my new friends, my new status.

Everything that has ever been, ends. And anything that hasn't ended yet, will. And that's a thought that terrifies me.

25

Derek drove around town aimlessly for an hour before we ended up at Sawhill, the park that separates his house and mine. We wanted to be away from school and closer to home. Whilst we drove he stayed silent, occasionally swearing under his breath every time someone cut him up, or when the traffic lights changed to red before he got there.

Only when we pulled up to the park and got out of the car did we start speaking, and he broke the silence with the only thing I really wanted to hear. "Let's go get Charlie." I nodded instantly.

We had pulled over on the side of Sawhill furthest from my house. It would've been quicker to jump back in and drive to my house to get Charlie, but I wanted to get out of the car and stretch my legs and I didn't even care that it was raining. Derek didn't seem to care either, or at least he didn't mention it. Together we walked over the rainsoaked grass towards my house. Because of the weather and the fact it was two o'clock on a Wednesday the park was almost empty. The park, which is basically just a large square of grass with a few play areas and too many trees, looked so different with no one around. It looked how it used to, years ago. Derek and I would come here every day during summer a few years ago, wanting to get out of the house and away from our families. We'd bring Charlie with us and we'd watch as he played on the swings, climb on the fences and jump around. It was great to watch because it's a time when Charlie was not limited by his deafness, he could be a normal kid when he was playing in the park.

Whilst watching him Derek and I would play cards, or throw a ball around even though we both hate sports. We'd talk about how great it was to be away from everyone at school. Mom let us go alone because she could see us from the kitchen window. It was my happy place for those days during summer, our happy place. And then everything changed.

I don't know whether it was because we were growing up or people were growing up around us, but the park changed. Howard T. Sawhill, after whom the park is named, was an old wealthy philanthropist who lived in our little old town his whole life, he personally paid for the preservation and upkeep of the park. Saying how he, like us, had the best days of his life on that park when he was a kid. He struck gold when he bought shares in a small electronics company that would later go multinational and multi-corporational and which in turn made him a multi-millionaire. Even though he made millions he stayed in our town because it was his home, he stayed in the same house and didn't spend a penny updating or upgrading it. Instead, he invested his money into our town and Howard T.

Sawhill Park was his most prized asset. It was put on the National Register of Historic Places and that was pretty much the biggest thing that has ever happened to this town. When Howard died and the money stopped, the park was repossessed by the council, it's given very, very minimal budget for upkeep. The grass is rarely cut and the broken swing sets have been that way since just after Howard died.

He loved this park and everything it represented, but after he died it went to shit. After it stopped being looked after, and the trees and the bushes grew tall and wild it became a hangout for the homeless, the drug dealers and the 'uncouth youth', as my Mom calls them. The wild and overgrown landscape gives good cover for people to do, uh, not legal things without being seen. We can no longer see the park from our kitchen window at home, because there are too many bushes in the way.

Mason organised a party in the park one time, and the place got trashed. I could still see remnants of the party that haven't been blown away by the wind or washed away in the rain. The vomit stains and cigarette butts have gone, but the fence that was ripped up as part of a drinking game. The keg is still at the park, nobody bothered taking it with them once it was empty. Underwear hangs out of bushes like fruit ready for picking. Beer bottles, discarded cigarettes, and condoms, both used and still wrapped are scattered all over. Memoirs from a great and historic night. To me, it was a send off to the park more than a party. The park means more to me than it does to a lot of my new friends.

That party was the night of my first real argument with Jenny. And it was so stupid. We'd agreed earlier in the day that we would meet there, she was going to get ready at Dana's house, and Derek and I were getting ready at his house. We got to the party when it was in mid-flow, most people there were already pretty wasted. Derek's parents' liquor cabinet was running low because 1) we were swiping at least one bottle every weekend and 2) Derek told me his Dad was drinking a lot more, so we didn't risk taking any from there, which meant that when we arrived and everyone else was wasted, we weren't.

The trees provided decent enough noise insulation as and blocked out the view of the park from the houses surrounding it, so we had no idea how wild it would be by the time we got there. The local residents probably knew that something was going on, but no one bothered reporting it. Everyone knew Sawhill was a shithole now and people generally tried to avoid it. We walked under the archway of trees that led to the park, with high hopes for what turned out to be a shitty night...

Mason had greeted us with two cups in each hand "Have you had an apple-and-pear cut Morgan?" he said and gestured towards my hair, he'd mastered the skill of carrying as many drinks as he could at once, negating the need for a second trip, but he still didn't have the hang of cockney rhyming slang. Derek and I necked one drink each whilst Mason downed the remaining two. Even though we were getting used to this lifestyle, Mason could still out drink us. Mason could out-drink anyone, and he never said no to a challenge. He's not exactly the biggest kid. I don't know how he does it. Rumour has it that Mason once outdrank an entire college football team, although another rumour has it that Mason started that rumour.

I once asked him why and how he could drink so much. His reply was solemn and made me wish I hadn't asked. "It must be in my DNA I guess." Everyone knew Mason's Dad was an alcoholic that beat Mason's Mom. Mr Ford is now locked up in a state prison somewhere, for a list of felonies probably as long as the list of people he's hurt. Mason is top of that list, and that's why he drinks. He answered my question without answering it, I never asked again.

Since his Dad got locked up and his Mom is always staying at her new boyfriend's, or working late, or drinking late, Mason always has the house to himself. Maybe that's why he throws so many parties, he hates an empty house.

We followed Mason to the centre of the park, the gentle thud of a bass was now escaping through the gaps in the trees. When we reached the source of the music, we saw the true chaos of what we had entered. There were bonfires, fireworks, traffic cones, traffic lights, motorbikes, car doors. A tree had been uprooted and was being used as a bench. People were skinny dipping in the fountain in the centre of the park. It amazed me that none of this carnage could be seen or heard from outside the park. Mason throws the best parties in the best locations, everyone knows that. He is the king of the rager, and that night was no exception.

Before I got too wasted I slumped off to find Jenny. She hadn't replied but it didn't take me long to find her. I walked down a short path, stepped over three or four unconscious seniors, dodged a flaming arrow that flew at my head height and entered a small clearing. I saw Jenny and Jordan stood close together, he was whispering something in her ear.

My animal instinct tore my body in half as I had a war with myself over the carnal fight or flight. I'd never won a fight with Jordan before, and I doubt this time would be any different. A lot had changed in the last few months, but one constant that always remained the same is that Jordan is a lot bigger than me and hits a lot harder than I ever could.

So, I ran. And I'm not embarrassed by that. In Biology we learnt about Darwinism and evolution, we learnt about food chains and how packs of lions hunt down gazelles whilst the gazelles chomp on grass and leaves. I'm sure Charles Darwin would agree that if a gazelle wants to survive, it isn't going to charge at a lion and punch it in the face. No matter how much the gazelle has changed in recent months, and a slightly drunk gazelle is even less useful.

Without stopping I ran back to Derek, I found him talking to Dana on one of the uprooted tree trunks. The smudges of colour on Derek's lips, a colour that almost perfectly matched Dana's lipstick, suggested that they'd been kissing and that I'd interrupted them. This had been happening more and more recently. It was becoming a habit. They'd both go to a party, make out, and when they'd see each other at school the next week they'd pretend nothing had happened.

I told them in a hushed and hurried tone what I'd just seen, and asked what they thought Jenny and Jordan could be speaking about.

"Go and talk to her and find out," Derek said. I wasn't sure whether that was his sincere advice or whether he just wanted to get rid of me so he could carry on with Dana. I suspected the latter.

"I'm sure it's nothing," Dana said. "It's not worth bringing up. They have a lot of the same friends, they're bound to run into each other. And who cares if they have a chat when they see each other, they did date for over a year!"

She had a point, so I told her that. "You've got a point, but still, do you reckon Jenny would be happy if I was being all close and friendly with my ex?"

"Yeah but—" Dana started to say.

"You don't have an ex," Derek finished her sentence.

They were right. I had never had a proper girlfriend before. Even though what they said and how they said it sounded harsh, I knew what my friends meant. I don't know much about the whole girlfriend thing, and I know even less about the ex-girlfriend thing. Being with Jenny is completely new to me, I don't know what would happen when, if, we broke up.

In the end, even though their advice was logical, correct, and with my best interests at heart, I ignored it. With a certain amount of Dutch courage, and by that I mean I went and got completely hammered beforehand, I confronted Jenny.

"What is it, Alex?" she said. Her voice was flat. She stared at me with a cold look that I hadn't seen before.

She stood in front of me with her hands entwined, I watched her twist the ring on her right index finger. I wondered where she got it. I'd never asked. Suddenly I wanted to know.

"Who gave you that ring?"

"What?" Jenny said. "Why does that – what do you mean?"

"The ring you're fiddling with. Who gave it to you?" My head was spinning. The campfire we were stood near threw light in my eyes. People talking and singing and dancing around it deafened me. My senses were all over the place.

"It was – uh – a birthday present, from an ex," she said. "I can't remember which one."

"You can't remember which ex? You've had that many?"

"I mean I can't remember which birthday," she snapped. "What's this about?"

"Him," I said, and she knew. She knew without me having to say anything. She knew I meant Jordan.

"What about him?"

"I saw you with him earlier, you looked…. Cosy."

"Are you fucking serious?" I recoiled at her curse. "Wow, Alex. I thought you were different. He was always getting jealous when we were together, I couldn't even look at another guy without him getting on my ass about it. I thought you were different but you're the same. You're all the fucking same." She turned around and started to walk off.

"Jenny, I…" I reached forward to grab her but tripped over my own feet and landed face first. The Dutch courage was failing me. A whimper escaped my lips. She turned to see what had happened but didn't stop walking.

That was my first, and so far only, argument with Jenny. The next day we ignored the elephant in the room, swept it under the rug and pretended it didn't happen. In the same way, Dana and Derek 'forgot' what happened between them that night, so did Jenny and I. But an elephant can't hide under a rug forever. Eventually, it's going to need to come up for air.

I carried on walking through Sawhill with Derek. With Derek at my side we walked past the remnants of the night, we walked past the tree stump Derek and Dana were sat on without so much as a flinch or a second glance from Derek. His elephant hadn't come out from under the rug yet either. I looked at the mess in sorrow. I grew up at Sawhill, to my friends it was just a new place to get drunk. To me, it's part of my home. When I drank it was a toast to the park, my park. I drank in memory of the days Derek and Charlie and I spent here as kids. I thought of the people that ruined my park, the ones I hated whilst growing up. I'd begun to realise that I am one of them.

26

Walking across the diameter of the park took a while; I'd forgotten how big it was. But at least the rain was stopping. I slid my key into the lock and turned, careful not to make a sound. I didn't want my Mom to hear we had got home. She may have got accustomed to me arriving home late, but I don't think she was ready for me to start getting home from school early.

I contemplated taking my shoes off, to quieten my footsteps, but decided against it. Derek waited outside whilst I crept around the house looking for Charlie. Luck was on my side, for once, Charlie was in the lounge alone.

"Where's Mom?" I signed to him, as he looked up at me. He answered by pointing up at the ceiling. She's in her room.

"Come with me," I told him, and he came with me without question or query. He stood up, and followed me to the door.

I knew Mom would freak out if she came down and found Charlie gone, so I had to tell her. I'd have to deal with her questions, but I decided that was something that could wait for later.

"MOM. I'm taking Charlie to the park. We'll be back later."

"WHAT DO YOU-" and we walked onto the porch and into the rain, closing the door behind us. Charlie grabbed my hand and followed me as I led him across the road and towards the park. I wished I'd grabbed a baseball or something for him to play with, but I knew that being out with me and Derek was enough for him. Even though he's grown up a lot since then, I was reminded of the kid he once was. He gripped my hand tight as we crossed the road.

I knew it was irresponsible taking him away from the house, he'd literally just got out of the hospital, but I wanted to see him. And I wanted to prove to my mum and dad that he wasn't a kid anymore, and that we didn't have to baby-proof the house.

For the next few hours, we were kids again, and we were indestructible. When we fell down in the wet mud we laughed, Derek slipped over and got covered in mud, I offered him my arm to help him get up, but he grabbed it and pulled me down into the mud with him. Charlie never got to experience life in England, not that he can remember at least, so I taught him some of the playground games I'd found out about. I left before I had even started school, so I never even learnt these games first hand, but I thought it might make him feel more at home here if he learnt them as well. We played tag and tig and British bulldog and hopscotch. I showed Charlie the pond, ignoring how similar it was to the one at Masons that may or may not have fish in it. Those few hours in that park with Derek and Charlie were better than any I spent at the party here not long ago. Hell, I had more fun here with them than I had had at any party. It felt like me. It felt real. Charlie was limitless again, not restricted by his lack of hearing. He was powerful, we all were.

The rain stopped shortly after we arrived, and the sun came out. In books, it's called pathetic fallacy, when the weather reflects the mood of the characters. I learnt that in English class. It was almost as if Mother Nature wanted us to have this day, and wanted it to be perfect. And you know what? It was. For those short few hours I ignored everything that had happened recently: I turned off my phone and turned off everything in my life that didn't include being here in this park with my two favourite people.

As it so often does, time caught up with us. I hadn't realised that it was starting to get late until I could no longer see my shadow. In complete harmony, mine and Charlie's stomachs rumbled. Derek wished me good luck and crossed the park to his house. It was time to take the kid home for dinner. It was time to face my Mom, she was bound to have questions.

And she did. Lots of them. She brought us crashing back to reality. She wanted to know why I thought it was acceptable to take Charlie and run, to blatantly disregard his safety and welfare and run off and take him somewhere so dangerous. I told her that it was the same park we used to play in when we were a lot smaller, we were fine.

"It is not the same place, it has changed. People have changed. You've changed. How could you put your brother in danger like that? Huh? How could you?"

"Sorry, Mom," was all I could say.

"Don't give me that. You're not sorry. Ever since you've been swanning off with your new mates and your girlfriend you've been like this. Getting hit by that bus was the worst thing that has happened to you. You're different. You used to be so sweet and thoughtful, but now you think it's acceptable to just take your brother to some drug den? You're grounded Alex. You're not allowed out. I will not take this. I will not have my child being put in danger. Not again."

At this point, I stormed upstairs. I'd been acting like a child with Derek and Charlie all afternoon, so I didn't even feel bad for throwing a temper tantrum and running off to my room. If my door had a lock I would have locked it, instead, I slammed my door and sat in front of it. Blocking anyone's entry.

My Mom was right, of course, I am different now. I'm not stupid. I can see that I've changed a lot, but I wouldn't agree that I've changed for the worse. Before the accident I was nothing, now I am something. Now I belong somewhere. I turned on my phone and checked my messages for the first time in hours. I ignored the texts and missed calls from my Mom and opened up the new message from Jenny.

"Do u need me? Come over after school if you want. Parents are at some conference as usual. Would be good to see you xx"

Without a second thought, I stood up and walked to the window, sliding it open once I reached it. I could've just walked out the front door, it would be less dramatic and less effort, but I didn't want to face my Mom again, not yet. And besides, I've snuck in enough times, it would be a nice change to sneak out once. With one leg on the trellis outside my window, I was frozen by the only thing that could have stopped me from leaving. The sound of Charlie's voice.

"Leks," he croaked.

Charlie can talk. He was five at the time of his accident so he could basically talk properly when it happened, and he still can, he just chooses not to. He doesn't like talking to people and not being able to hear what they respond. That's why we all learned sign-language. He spoke to communicate whilst Mom was teaching him how to sign, but he's barely done it since, he only does it when he deems it really necessary.

When he was very young he struggled to pronounce my name fully, Alex became Aleks which became Leks. It was what he would call me. It felt weird hearing it out loud again.

I turned to face him and started to retract my leg from the open window. He opened his mouth again but I put my finger to my lips, shushing him.

"It's okay buddy, I'm here. I'm staying," I signed. I walked over to the lamp that stood in the corner of my room, turned it on and carried it to the centre of my bedroom, it was now several inches shorter than me. Charlie knew what I had in mind. He walked over to my bed and grabbed my duvet, and together we draped the duvet over the lamp. One by one we crawled into our little tee-pee, we were both too big for it now. It was something we hadn't done in years. His feet stuck out of the side and so did most of my shins. But thanks to the light inside our teepee it was a place we could have a secret conversation, hidden from the outside world. Just me and him. Again. We talked with our hands for the rest of the evening. At one point Mom came in and shouted for us to come to dinner. Charlie didn't hear her, of course, and I pretended not to. She was part of the outside world that was being blocked by the protective shield of our duvet/teepee.

Eventually, Charlie fell asleep on my legs, I was uncomfortable and I doubted I could fall asleep in that position. I was wrong.

27

The light rolled in through my still-open window and woke me up. I was glad Charlie had stopped me when he did, but I still needed to see Jenny. I reminded myself out loud that I'd see her at school.

"School. Fuck," I said, thankful that Charlie couldn't hear me swear. Looking at my watch I swore again, I was going to be late. I crawled out of the teepee and stood up, careful not to wake Charlie. Even though I didn't have time to do it, I took the duvet off the lamp, picked Charlie up and carried him to my bed. He stirred slightly but settled once I'd placed him on my duvet-less bed. I grabbed the duvet and threw it on his sleeping figure. With Charlie safely asleep I was free to charge around my room getting ready, knowing no amount of noise would wake him.

With only one arm in the t-shirt I'd chosen, I charged down the stairs, picking up Mom's car keys off the hook as I passed. "Mom I'm taking the car, or I'm going to be late," I shouted into the general direction I thought she would be.

"YOU DON'T SEEM TO MIND MISSING SCHOO—"

"Not now Mom," I said, jogging out my house and onto the porch. After fumbling with the lock on the car for far too long, I managed to jimmy the door open. Having already lost too much time I drove too fast towards school, it had rained overnight but wasn't any more, the roads were slippery, dangerous. I passed Derek's house on the way and was thankful that he'd been there when I needed him. Derek was one of the only things that hadn't changed about my life since the accident. Everything else was new and different and sometimes exciting, but Derek was still Derek, just like Charlie was still Charlie.

I thought back to what Derek had said a while back: that he expects us to end up back at his house on Saturday nights soon enough. I wondered if he still meant that. His life had changed, for the better, just as mine had. He was like me before, and we're like each other now. We fit in pretty well, but that made me wonder why we didn't before. Surely Derek would prefer to spend his weekends attached to Dana's lips than playing Quake with me.

I'm lucky that I have Jenny, and I'm going to do whatever it takes to keep her. Saving her is what brought us together, and I'd begun to think that maybe that's what I had to do to keep her. For the rest of the journey to school I cleared my head and brainstormed. I perfected my new plan throughout the entire day, barely listening to whatever I was being taught.

In my last class of the day, I sent two text messages. One to Jenny asking her to meet me at the front of school so we could drive home together. The other text I sent to Derek, telling him I needed a hand with something and that he should meet me by my locker after final bell. He agreed straight away, replying with "Whatever it is, count me in. Unless it's something highly illegal. My ass couldn't handle prison."

Jenny responded less enthusiastically with "Sure, ok xx"

Derek beat me to my locker after school. "You know, depending on what type of illegal it was, I might be alright with it," he said, a knowing smile on his face.

"Good to know," I said. "Because what I'm about to ask you to do does break the law." I grabbed Mom's car keys from my pocket and chucked them to him.

"Driving isn't illegal, Alex."

"Technically you're not insured on my Mom's car so it would be illeg— you know what, nevermind. Just listen to my plan, and then you can tell me if it's a type of illegal you're okay with."

"Sir, yes, sir," he said, saluting me. I gave him a one-fingered salute back.

—

"Hey, you," I said as I took Jenny's hand five minutes later, taking care to position myself on her left-hand side. "Sorry I'm late, I had to go grab a book from my locker."

"It's okay. How was your day? Where did you go yesterday? I tried texting you but..."

"I'm fine, everything's fine, I just had to clear my head, you know, with Charlie and everything. We just went over to Sawhill and played on the swings and looked at the fishpond for a bit."

"I thought fishponds were our thing?" she teased and leaned in to kiss me on the cheek. "What's the plan then? Back to mine?"

"Yeah, sounds good," I said whilst looking around for Derek. Jenny and I walked to the front of the school together, hand in hand. Rain was pouring down, and we avoided the puddles. The soggy grass glistened, then spat mud when stepped on. We got to the end of the path, ready to cross the road.

Derek appeared far to my left. His knuckles were visible above the steering wheel of my Moms car, but his face wasn't. He'd hidden it with his coat. He adjusted his speed as he calculated how long it would take for us to reach the kerb.

The car sped up and time slowed down. He started to skid through the puddles, the tyres spraying water everywhere. I reacted the second my Mom's car mounted the sidewalk.

I pulled Jenny's hand with my right arm and spun around her, spinning her into an embrace with my back to the kerb. My right hand grabbed the back of her neck and pulled her face into my chest as we span away from the car. I could almost feel the front bumper graze the back of my right leg as it skidded past us and slipped back onto the road. Derek had gotten closer than we'd planned.

A few moments later I leant back and looked down at Jenny, her face was still. She looked shocked, but not in a bad way.

"What is it with you and this kerb? You're a curse, I swear," I said, breaking the silence that hung in the air.

"Fucking hell, Morgan." Mason's was the first voice I heard. "Again?" I looked at him and smirked. What had just happened had attracted quite a crowd. I couldn't help but feel smug.

"I don't... I didn't... You're always saving me," Jenny said.

"It was easier this time," I said. "I must be getting better at it."

"Who the fuck was driving that car?" Mason asked, and he began to charge down the road after my Mum's car.

"Don't worry about it, Mase," I said. "The roads are soaking wet. It's not his fault."

"You saw it was a man?" Mason asked. "What did he look like?"

"Uh, no, I'm just guessing. Look, honestly it's fine. We're fine. Nobody got hurt."

"...this time," Jenny whispered, but I don't think she meant for me to hear it, so I didn't respond.

"Can we get out of here? I'm soaked" I said to Jenny. The rain hadn't slowed down.

"Yeah come on, let's get my car," she suggested. I nodded and followed her across the road, avoiding the puddles Derek had just driven through, though they were now considerably smaller.

We got into Jenny's car and she looked at me.

She had eyes you could swim in and she was staring straight at me, and everything was suddenly worthwhile.

We sat there for a bit while she caught her breath. When we'd both calmed down, she put the car into reverse, whacked the heating on full and backed out of the parking space. Her awareness of what was around her was incredible considering she wasn't looking where she was going at all. She paid minimal attention to the road and kept stealing glances at me whenever she could, it was almost as if she was checking to make sure I hadn't floated away or something.

We arrived at her big, empty house and she told me to take my clothes off so she could put them in the wash. I stripped down to my underwear and handed her my clothes, "Pass me those too, they'll be wet as well," she said, nodding towards my boxers. I obliged. She instructed me to go have a shower whilst she sorted my clothes out. She rushed around the house with her hands full of my wet clothes as I showered. When she was done, she met me in the bathroom, grabbed my hand and led me to her bedroom. Within seconds I wasn't the only one not wearing anything. Our clothes didn't return to our bodies for the rest of the evening.

28

Staring up at the dolphins on the ceiling of Jenny's room I was in a state of total bliss. What had happened the night before was everything I had ever imagined it to be, and I'd imagined it a lot of times. In fact, it was better. The icing on the proverbial cake was when Jenny stopped and looked me in the eyes, giving me another chance to swim in the blue. She sighed "I love you, Alex." Her sudden confession left me in shock. It took me far too long to say it back, but I did. Because I did. I do. I loved her so much, it feels impossible. Before the accident, I didn't know I was capable of this, capable of an all-consuming passion for someone else. In my life, I had never allowed anyone to get close enough to let myself feel this way, but there was something different about Jenny.

Before things changed I thought that I loved her, but now I knew. I knew because I felt it in every breath that I take and every beat of my heart. It wasn't a TV type of love, not the type of love where everything is perfect and no one ever gets hurt, it was real, and broken, and patchy. But it was real. And now it was whole because I knew that she felt it too.

The things I love the most were the things that no one else noticed, I love how when she yawns her mouth opens so wide it looks like she was trying to swallow a tennis ball. When she kisses me I can feel the edges of her mouth curl up into a smile. When she strokes my hand with her thumb she only strokes in counter-clockwise circles. She's the only person I know who texts using her index fingers, and not her thumbs. When she eats a hamburger she decomposes it and eats the pieces one by one. Top bun, burger, bottom bun. When she sleeps she puts her arms around herself in an embrace, like she doesn't want to be alone. But she doesn't have to be alone anymore.

She was asleep with her head on my chest, my arm around her neck. My left hand was around her bare back, pulling her in tighter. My right hand was tracing back and forward over the skin between her hip and her ribs.

The dolphins shone brightly above us, they probably would've been keeping me awake if I was trying to sleep. But I couldn't sleep even if I wanted to. Sleeping leads to waking up, and if I wake up then I might realise that it was just a dream. I led there in silence whilst Jenny slept, just listening to her breathe. Scared of waking her, I stayed still, matching her breaths with mine, trying my best to avoid any movements that would stir her from her angelic sleep. I wondered if life ever got any better than this, and I doubted it. I can't imagine a time when anything would ever be as perfect.

I led there motionless and watched the sunrise through the window in Jenny's room. We hadn't gotten around to closing the curtains. The sun was the only indicator of what time it was, there was no clock in Jenny's room and I'd taken my watch off. I didn't know where my phone was. My internal body clock told me it was about 7, which meant I'd been awake for over 24 hours now. I decided to give it 20 minutes before waking Jenny up, I was okay with missing school, especially if the alternative was staying in bed with Jenny, but I knew that with being head of pretty much every school committee we had, she had a lot of stuff to do before the end of year.

Gently, I woke her up sooner than I'd told myself I would. She stirred and opened her eyes slowly. For a second she looked frightened and I was worried she'd forgotten that I was there. But then a smile formed on her face and she leant up to kiss me.

"Good morning," she breathed.

"Hey, you," I said to her, pulling away from her kiss, feeling endlessly thankful for every decision I had ever made. Together we got out of bed, showered and dressed. We chatted mindlessly about nothing important. Her smile mimicked mine.

Whilst she finished getting ready I rummaged around the cupboards in the kitchen for something to eat. Living in a no-parent household had taken its toll on the cupboard stocks. In the end, I found two dessert waffles with honey for each of us.

In the months we'd been together I've never known her to eat at home. She'd either eat at mine, or

Dana's or grab something when she's out. I know she tries to avoid being in the house as much as she can.

She takes up as many responsibilities as she can just to keep her busy. The only time we're ever at her house for long periods of time is when it's her turn to host a party, on the odd occasion Mason's house isn't available.

I'd recently realised that a lot of my friends come from broken homes. Mason's parents are split up, his Dad's in prison. Dana's Dad died when she was very young, she lives with her Mom and her younger sister. From what Derek's told me, Dana did most of the parenting when it came to her sister, she helped her with her homework and made her a packed lunch. She did everything her Mom was supposed to do but was too busy working three jobs just to pay for the food that Dana put in her sister's lunch box. Dana's mom remarried, so it's a bit better now, but growing up was hard.

Jenny's parents are still around, in theory. They're absentee parents just as much as Dana, or Mason's parents are. I suddenly appreciated my, somewhat dysfunctional, family more than I had done in a long time.

Jenny's Mom has the image that they're still one big happy family, and on the rare occasion they're all in town together, the faux show she puts on embarrasses Jenny. I'd only seen Jenny's parents once since they visited me in hospital. But the next time Jenny introduced me as her boyfriend, not just some kid that saved her life.

Luck had it that Mr and Mrs Evans' coinciding court dates meant that they were both at home at the same time, Leanne insisted that Jenny invited me around for a family meal so we could all get to know each other. Considering Jenny had learnt to deal with my Mom, I owed her the same. So I agreed to it.

It was a train wreck.

I could tell from the look of contempt on my girlfriend's face that she could sense the false sincerity as much as I could. Leanne tried, I'll give her that much credit. When I arrived at the door they all greeted me, together, with Jenny in the middle and her parents left and right of her, each with a hand on her shoulder. They stepped towards me, standing in front of their daughter. Leanne was a carbon copy of her daughter – or maybe that should be the other way around, looking at Leanne was like looking into the future. My future.

Leanne's hair dropped onto her shoulders the same way Jenny's did, her eyes were the same shape, only not quite as blue as her daughters. Leanne wore a red dress and Mr Evans ("I insist you call me Steve!") wore a dark suit jacket with dark shoes and jeans, an American flag pinned to his lapel.

His tie was a colour so similar to Leanne's dress it looked as if they were prom dates that had colour coordinated their outfits to match each other. I felt very much underdressed in dark jeans and a white shirt I stole from my Dad. Steve extended his hand and I shook it. I'd spent the day practising handshakes with Derek. I hugged Leanne and recited, with perfect inflexion, a line I'd also been practising all day, "Thank you so much for having me, your house is lovely."

Derek told me I should say "your home is lovely," but that would be a lie. Not because it wasn't lovely, but because it wasn't a home. So I went with "house".

"Oh thank you, Alex that's very kind," Leanne said. "Perhaps we could show you around later."

Truthfully, I'd probably spent more time there than she had over the last few months, I doubted I'd need the tour. I didn't tell her that though, of course. Instead, I just said what you're supposed to say in that situation: "Oh that would be lovely!"

Mr Evans left his wife's side and walked around me to close the door, ushering me inside.

"Follow Jenny into the dining room, dear. I've just got to finish up with dinner, it won't be long. Steve, darling, could you give me a hand?" Leanne said. I started walking in the direction of where I knew the dining room to be, but Jenny grabbed my hand and pulled me in the other direction.

"They've moved it," she said, visibly annoyed. Soon, as we walked under the arch to the room, I saw why they'd moved it. The small yet elegant dining table I had become used to in Jenny's house had been replaced by a monstrous, yet still elegant, mahogany dining table that could easily seat 15 people around it.

"I guess..." Jenny began, but she didn't have to explain. I got it. Mr and Mrs Evans wanted to give the impression that they had massive family dinners around this table, and that jokes were shared and wine was spilt. But this table was brand new. It may as well have still had the price tag on it. You could tell it had never been used for any big family dinners. It didn't have scuff marks or stains or chips in the wood. It was brand new and untouched, just like everything else in the Evans house.

Every chip or scratch on the dining table in my house tells a different story, holds a different memory of a different family dinner gone wrong. There's a significant dent in the middle of our table from the Thanksgiving where my Dad went to pick up the dish the turkey was on so he could carve it, but he didn't realise how hot the plate was. He dropped the plate and the turkey right into the middle of the table. In almost slow motion the plate rolled off the table and smashed. We spent the rest of Thanksgiving in the emergency room as my Dad got his burns attended to and my Mom picked shards of china out of her bare feet.

It was a disaster but I remember that Thanksgiving more than any I've had since we moved here, I remember laughing about it for days afterwards, and we still laugh about it now even if we didn't laugh at the time. Charlie finds it hilarious that we ended up ordering a pizza for Thanksgiving dinner, and so did the delivery man as he arrived with our pizza. He told us that it wasn't at all uncommon for people to order pizza on Thanksgiving. He said people either 1) can't cook, 2) won't cook, 3) cook but burn it, 4) argue over the cooking, or 5) cook perfectly but drop it on the floor and spend most of the evening in the emergency room.

The Evans' table had no stories to tell, no memories to share other than memories of its journey from the showroom to the new dining room.

The whole meal felt very false, the food was incredible but Jenny later told me that the home cooked dinner was in fact cooked by a catering company and dropped off just before I arrived. She said she doubted that her Mom would even know how to turn on the oven, she's used it so infrequently. The conversation felt nearly as faked as the 'home-cooked' food. Leanne laughed too hard and said too much, she asked too many questions and acted as if she was genuinely interested in my answers. Steve tried to play the protective Dad card but he wasn't fooling anyone, he asked about my car and my driving experience and hoped that I was keeping his precious daughter safe, I didn't mention that it was normally Jenny who drove us places, and she was a great driver.

The only part of the evening that felt genuine, other than the goodbye, was when we talked about the 'accident'. About saving Jenny's life. They had their flaws, and they weren't going to have books written on their immaculate parenting technique, that's for sure, but when they asked about it and said how grateful they were that I was there, they seemed like they meant it. I took solace from that and hoped Jenny did too. I told them about how in that moment Jenny was helpless, she didn't see it coming but I did, and if there was something I could do to help her, I was going to do it, and so I did.

"It didn't take much thought really," I told them. "It was just an instinct."

We'd come a long way since then. Strangely, shouting "Bus" at her before pushing her out the way was the first time I'd ever said anything to Jenny. I'd thought about it a lot, but was always too intimidated. And then, just a few months later, I found myself being introduced to her parents as her boyfriend. It was surreal.

Jenny told them about the other times I had saved her – the mugging and the car – and they were in awe, and thanked me again. Profusely. Their thanks was real, but much like everything else that had happened that evening, what they were thanking me for was completely fake.

May

29

The arrival of May meant that all seniors entered finals mode. Especially those of us who had college placements depending exam results. I'd be lying if I said that academia and grades were still my number one priority. Before I developed overnight infamy, I'd applied myself to my highest potential because I had no excuse not to. I studied for tests because I wanted to get a spot in a decent college and get away from St. Francis, Kansas. But I was no longer sure if I wanted to get away. My new list of priorities would greatly differ to my list before the accident.

Don't get me wrong, I wasn't failing. A mixture of natural intelligence and the hard work I'd put in during my freshman and junior years of high school had kept my GPA afloat in my, well, less dedicated times. But I'd been given no choice but to study. Jenny, Derek, Dana, and even Mason, who never takes anything seriously, were all locked up indoors up to their noses in books and revision notes.

That's what brought me to the library on a sunny Saturday, with a laptop case full of good intentions.

The faculty had made the decision to keep Williamsburg open at weekends to allow students use of the library and its other facilities. The student council – so, Jenny – had campaigned for it because buying your own version of the books is ridiculously expensive, and the grades of the less fortunate among the student body shouldn't have to suffer because they can't afford textbooks.

Whatever the reason for it, I was glad the library opened at weekends. I couldn't study at home. It was too loud. Mom and Dad were constantly shouting at each other. On this rare occasion, it made me thankful Charlie is deaf. He doesn't need to hear them going at each other like that. In a twisted way, I envied him for not being able to hear it. The argument is the same as it always had been: Dad says Mom needs to get a job because he has to work double shifts to pay for Charlie's hospital bills. Mom remains adamant that she needs to be at home with Charlie 24/7. She's wrong, of course, but she'd never admit it.

Being part of my new social group has made me realise that high school is bearable, for some. Charlie could fit in at any regular school. Before I came into this group I would've said the opposite, that high school is a place for narcissists and bullies and to avoid it at all costs, but since I've seen how much love my friends have for Charlie, I've changed my mind. He's infectious, and he'd cope at regular school no problem. He might need an interpreter, sure, and that would cost either the school, or us, a fair amount, but if he was at school full time then Mom could get a job and more than cover the costs of an interpreter.

He could get a better, proper, education. His education will always be limited because, as brilliant of a woman as she is, my Mom isn't a natural teacher; she doesn't have the patience or the knowledge to adequately teach Charlie what he needs to know. He's not unintelligent, but he's probably behind in his academic development compared to other non-homeschooled thirteen-year-olds. Dad knows that, and it comes up in their arguments. A lot. Mom argues that she's doing the best she can in a bad situation, which Dad, and I, agree that she is but we, as a family, can do better for him. But still, they have the same argument every day.

Mom blames Dad because he made us move to America. If we didn't move then 1) Charlie's accident never would've happened and 2) if it did, free healthcare would mean Dad wouldn't have to work his ass off to pay for everything, and he could be home more, and 3) Mom could have more of a life herself. They're arguing more and more since Charlie went into hospital again. Thankfully though, it didn't seem like Charlie would have any more long-term problems because of the latest accident.

As I sat down looked around at the other sorry souls that had traded their Saturdays for solitude. Meowth was there, tearing his hair out over a biology book. Mason had told me that Meowth's parents would cut his allowance if he didn't get into college. I've seen the car he drives, and if I was at risk of losing that I'd probably be tearing my hair out too.

A few of the Fists littered a table to the right of me. Watching them surround a book whilst scratching their heads made me picture a group of cavemen who had just come across an iPad and had absolutely no idea what to do with it. The cavemen probably had a higher chance of getting into college than Fists Two through Six. I chuckled aloud at the image I'd created in my head, I got a few funny looks and a "shhhhh".

Jordan was basically guaranteed a spot in college, of course. His talent on the football pitch and his father's connections gave him a guaranteed place at any school that had a sports team. He basically only had to show up to his exams and write his name on the paper and he'd get into college.

He'd been almost non-existent in my life since I pretty much took over his. I know he's pissed that I took his girlfriend and friendship group, but he leaves me alone as long as I stay out of his way. Losing Jenny is the highest form of punishment I could ever inflict on him, and I saw no need to take away his future as well as his past.

We hadn't completely swapped social positions though. He was still the captain of the most successful football team in the history of our school, and that comes with a certain amount of popularity. But he's dropped, and I've climbed. His old friends, my current friends, resent him because he had this violent streak that they didn't know about.

Most people found out about everything not long after I'd told Jenny. It spread like a bush fire, as most things do in this school. Fortunately for Jordan, it stayed away from the faculty. If they found out, he'd be out of school and out of college for sure. Derek had suggested we tell the school and put the last nail in the coffin and get rid of him for good. I told him we weren't going to be nailing anyone and he should stop using so many clichés. To that, he made a clichéd sex joke about nailing, and I rolled my eyes.

Only when Meowth stood up, knocking over his chair as he did so, did I wake up from my near slumber. I thought the splinters in my ass would stop me from sleeping, but they didn't stop me from daydreaming. I'd been there fifteen minutes already and hadn't yet opened a book. I walked over to Meowth and helped him pick up the books he'd spilt.

"Thank you, Alex," he said as I bent to pick up his B2 textbook. "How is the studying going?"

"Pretty shit, not gonna lie," I responded. "There are so many places I would rather be right now than here. And so many things I would rather be doing."

"Damned right," he said. "I've been studying very hard all week. We should have a night off. I think we'll have a party at my house tonight. Bring your friends and your beer." I gave him a smile and he returned it. It wasn't an invitation, and I didn't have much of a choice. He knew I'd be there.

Suddenly, with something to look forward to, a day of studying seemed a lot more manageable. Meowth walked out of the library with a wave and I walked back to my table, grabbed my phone and sent a quick group text. "Short notice I know, Meowth's having a 'thing' tonight. Who's in?"

Derek replied first: "I can't come. But can you look after D for me?"

"This is a group text, Derek, I can see what you reply you idiot." Dana replied, followed shortly after by a semi-colon and closed parenthesis so he knew she was joking.

"Uhm, yeah I'm in I guess xx," Jenny replied 15 minutes later. "Could use a break xx"

"Don't get too excited, you'll wet yourself," Derek text back.

And that was that. My day went from monotony to anarchy within a moment. I was excited.

30

Jenny picked me up at nine and we rode in her car to Meowth's. As usual, we could hear the party before we saw the house – which was even more impressive considering you can't really call Meowth's place a house. It was more of a palace. Calling it a house would be an insult to its grandeur. You could probably have fit three of my house inside of Meowth's and you'd still have room for a medium-sized parking garage, and the garden's grounds were just as splendorous.

As far as I can recall, Meowth never expressed any interest in sport of any kind, but dotted around his house, in plural, were tennis courts, swimming pools, basketball hoops, batting cages, and putting greens. I swear I even saw a half pipe built into the foundations.

I wondered out loud how it was possible we'd never been to Meowth's for a party before, Mason threw wild parties but his house didn't come close to comparing to this one.

"Asmir's parents are pretty strict – rich people generally are," Jenny told me. She was the only person

I knew that called Meowth by his real name. "They don't go away often so his house is never free."

"Your parents are rich, but we have parties at yours all the time," I said.

"They are not ri—" she started to say, but I raised my eyebrows and she stopped. "Okay they are, but they don't know we have parties, do they?"

"Fair point," I said, and I took her hand and together we walked into the house.

"Dana said she'd be here by now, shall we go find her?" Jenny asked. I nodded and we set off to find Dana.

We didn't find Dana for a long time. The place was full when we got there and more people were arriving by the minute. Apparently, everyone needed a night off from studying. A house as big as Meowth's needed a lot of people to fill it, and Williamsburg was certainly giving it a go.

People that arrived before us littered the floor and the stairs and the tables. I hadn't seen Meowth yet. Actually, I hadn't seen many people I recognised. One of Jenny's Cheerfollowers was there with her boyfriend, and she told us that Meowth had invited a friend from the school across town, and he'd gone on to invite most of his school.

It seemed pretty much every teenager in town interested in underage drinking and narcotics was there. Jenny and I walked through the maze of bodies hand in hand so we didn't lose each other.

People forced drinks into our spare hands when they saw we were drinkless. We weren't allowed to pass until we'd finished our drinks. It was like a real-life version of the worst video game ever: to advance on our quest we had to drink our way through the frothy beer fountain, which made advancing on our quest thereafter slightly more wobbly.

One challenge Jenny and I faced on our quest to find Dana was adequately described 'Puff and blow'. It was a game coined by one of the kids from the school from the other side of town. It involved a great deal of puff and a lesser amount of blow. I don't remember the rules.

We passed over what had been coined 'Smoke Mountain' as we navigated up the stairs – marble and spiral, of course. Portraits and vases hung in and on the crevices that climbed the wall with us. An oil painting of Meowth had been phallically vandalised. Away from, not into. Thankfully.

Once we reached the top of the stairs a guy came storming around the corner out of the blue, unsighted and ran straight into a fat guy in front of us on the stairs. The guy in front let out a scream as he began to tumble backwards towards us. I saw it coming just in time. I grabbed Jenny and span us out the way of the leaning tower of Pizza-gut that was tumbling toward us. He fell on his back below the step we were standing on mere seconds ago.

"That would've hurt," I said. Jenny looked up at me and stared into my eyes. And there was blue. Only blue.

"Come on," I said. "Dana."

"Dana," she repeated.

"There were so many people. So many. Everywhere," I told the police officer. "We searched for her the whole night but we couldn't find her. When we found her she was in the bedroom with him. She wasn't conscious. He wasn't either." I couldn't say his name. I didn't know his name.

We found her eventually. They say that what you're searching for is always in the last place you look, but that's a bollocks saying because you're not going to carry on looking after you find it, are you? We walked into one of the seemingly infinite number of bedrooms in the Persian palace and saw Dana on the bed.

He, whoever he was, was passed out on the floor.

This time I reacted. I did what I should have done when I found Charlie under my parent's blankets, my phone was in my hand before my brain had had time to process what I was seeing.

"Tell everyone to get out," I said to Jenny as I dialled 911. "The police are on the way." It was 3am. It took us almost six hours to find her. We went to look for her right away. But got distracted. And drunk.

She stared at Dana, in shock. "NOW," I screamed. She obeyed. The police were going to know that there was a massive underage party happening, but that did not matter. Dana mattered. She needed help and I didn't care who went to jail to get her that help. I was not going to let down someone close to me when they need me most. Not again.

31

"I told you to look after her," Derek screamed at me. People were looking. My head was hurting. "Where the fuck were you?"

"She said she'd meet us there," I said. "She must have got there a while before us, and we went straight to look for her as soon as we got there." We were stood in the hallway outside Dana's hospital room. She'd been taken straight there to have her stomach pumped.

"You clearly didn't go straight there, you were wasted. You both were." He was angry, but he was right. "You must have stopped to get drunk and then decided to go and find her. Meanwhile my girlfriend was off having her drink spiked by some college guy."

"She's not your girlfriend," I reminded him.

"She may as well be. She's the most important thing to me now that you've fucked off with your own life," he screamed. This hurt me more than he'd ever know. It hurt mostly because I knew it was true. It's not like I'd ignored him since I got together with Jenny. He comes to all the same parties that we do, we still eat lunch together, there are just more people around us than there used to be. The time we spent together at Sawhill with Charlie is the only time in recent memory that we'd been us again, like before things changed, when it was Alex and Derek against the rest of the world.

"That's not true," I denied, even though I agreed with him. Jenny had driven Dana's mom and stepdad home to pick up some supplies for Dana. I was glad Jenny wasn't there to hear this.

"You know it is. You only have time for me when you want help with one of your crackpot schemes to stop Jenny from leaving you." I hated arguing with Derek. He knew me better than anyone did, and he knew what he could say to hurt me. I couldn't respond directly to that comment, I didn't know what to say. Instead, I changed the subject, slightly.

"Let's just be thankful that she's alright," I said. "It's happened now, but it could have been a lot worse."

We were told by the police that the college guy, whose name we knew only as Joe, was challenged by his friends to kiss someone at the party as some sort of twisted initiation. Nobody knew why the college guys were at Meowth's house or who invited them, they just showed up. When Dana brushed off Joe's initial advances, Joe seemed to back off. After she left Joe she went and stood with a few of the followers.

Somehow, and we don't know how, one of Joe's friends spiked her drink. Dana excused herself from the pack and stumbled to the bathroom, people saw her stumble off and lose her footing but everyone just assumed she was wasted like everyone else at the party. She didn't make it to the bathroom. With her drink in her hand she stumbled into the first room she saw, needing a soft place to lie down, her head spinning. She put her drink on the floor and collapsed onto the bed. Joe's friends pushed him into the room after her.

In the end, what saved Dana was that Joe got nervous. "He's not a malicious predator," the police officer had told us. "He's a dumb kid who got dared by his friends to do something stupid."

After he followed her into the room he got scared. The light from the hallway had lit up the room, and he saw Dana on the bed and a drink on the floor. He'd said it was too dark in there for him to realise that she was unconscious. To calm his nerves he picked up Dana's drink and downed it in one. Joe didn't know his friends had spiked her. He passed out almost instantly.

This story was told to us by the police, Dana herself had no idea what had happened. She woke up in the hospital with Derek holding her hand. I looked on from outside the room, Jenny was by my side, her face the palest I'd ever seen it. We felt each other's guilt. The police were in Joe's room when Dana woke up.

He said he didn't know that the drink had been spiked, and by speaking to him the police seemed to genuinely believe him. He said he didn't know who did it but he would provide the police with the names of the people he was with at the party.

He said he didn't see her stumbling and didn't realise that something was wrong. His frat brothers just pushed him into the room and told him to go in and flirt with her. Although nothing happened, he said he wanted to see Dana to apologise. The police forbade it, and if they hadn't, Derek would have.

Eventually, it was decided that, because nothing actually happened, Joe would go unpunished by law. He'd passed out before he'd even made it to Dana asleep on the bed. His fraternity, on the other hand, would be getting a visit from the police.

Jenny and I were pardoned for being drunk under the age of 21 because of the circumstances, and the police had more pressing matters to deal with as a result of that party. The officer in charge came and found me and assured me I did the right thing by phoning them. He told me if the drug is left in the system for too long the consequences could've been much more severe. That didn't matter to Derek.

"It's your fault," he said. "If you'd looked after her like you said you would we wouldn't be here. She wouldn't be in that bed. She wouldn't have had to have her stomach pumped just now."

Meowth was in a jail cell. He was one of the few that didn't run from the house. Jenny and I stayed for obvious reasons, but he stayed because it was his house and his party and he had to own up to that. His charges included distribution of alcohol to minors, disturbing the peace, destruction of property, being drunk and disorderly, and obstructing the truth from a police officer.

His parents will hire a lawyer expensive enough to get him off with a warning, but any punishment the police could give him would be nothing compared to the wrath his parents would bestow upon him when they came home to find that their baroque crystal chandelier was used as a tyre swing.

Nobody else knew the real reason the party got busted. Everyone assumed a neighbour had called the cops because of the noise.

Meowth's party went down in Williamsburg history; it was the milestone that all future parties were measured again. "Yeah that party was good, but it was no Meowth" was a phrase that would be forever used to describe a party in my town. Eventually, that phrase was shortened to "no Meowth." A phrase used to describe anything of slightly below awesomeness. Lunch specials in the school cafeteria were described as "no Meowth" when they were good, but not great.

A sports team's performance that was just below perfect was no Meowth. To everyone but us that party was notorious for all the right reasons, no one would forget it for years to come. The four of us couldn't wait to forget it. It was a near miss, in the end, we were lucky, but it served as a reminder of our carelessness.

"We're done, Alex," Derek spat. "Let me know when you start thinking of someone other than yourself." He turned and walked into Dana's room and resumed his post at her bedside. I walked outside and waited for Jenny.

"He's just mad at you because he wasn't there to help her," Jenny assured me. I'd got in her car after she'd returned with Dana's parents. We swapped places: they got out of the car and I got in. I'd told Jenny about everything Derek had said to me. Well, everything except the things that involved her.

Meeting Dana's parents for the first time under these circumstances felt wrong, our after-hours club had a strict rule that parents were not to know what happened when we partied. We had our fun and it was always cleared up before parents heard about it. It was different with Meowth. He was willing to bear the brunt of his actions. He's a bigger man than me.

"How've they taken it?" I said, motioning towards Dana's parents as we pulled away from the visitor drop off bay.

"I think they're more happy she's okay than mad she got into that situation in the first place," Jenny said. "If that makes sense."

"Totally," I said, glaring out of the window. Houses flashed past as we drove through town. It started to rain. Raindrops overtook my vision. It took me a while to realise that the raindrops were tears. I was crying. Jenny grabbed my hand so I would turn to face her. She looked me in the eye and there was blue again, and it didn't matter that Derek hated me and it didn't matter that Dana was in hospital and Meowth was in jail because there was blue in the world again.

There was movement at the edge of the blue, and maybe it was because I was becoming accustomed to disaster but I saw the movement before Jenny did.

Woof.

I ripped my hand from her grip and grabbed the steering wheel. I tore it towards me, then pushed it away from me again. Jenny slammed on the brakes as I finished my manoeuvre. I turned around and looked in the eyes of the dog we'd just narrowly avoided hitting. It was frozen in the middle of the road, eyes transfixed on Jenny's car. There were no other vehicles on the road. Nothing else could hurt us. Not now. We waited for the dog to move first. Waited for it to blink to prove it was okay.

It moved. And we breathed.

"Are you okay to drive?" I asked Jenny. She looked in shock. Her chest was puffing in time with the rhythm of her breath.

"I'm fine," she said. Her breathing slowed. "Is the dog okay?"

"Seems like it. It ran off pretty quick. You sure you're okay?"

"I'm fine, let's just get home," she argued her point when I questioned her on it. She was positive she was going to be okay. She didn't take her eyes off the road once and she barely spoke.

Whatever had just happened, it took my mind off Derek and Dana, if only for a minute. For that I was thankful. But after a while Derek drifted to the forefront of my mind. I didn't want to say much out loud because Jenny was really trying to focus on the road.

When we parked outside my house I took my opportunity to speak. "Do you think he'll forgive me?" I said.

"Of course he will Alex," she said. "When Dana gets out of hospital and this has all blown over, you'll go right back to what you used to be."

She didn't know it, but what we used to be wasn't what we were before Meowth's party. We used to be different. The only exciting thing about Saturday nights for us used to be choosing which pizza topping we were going to order.

A year ago the thought of spending Saturdays in Persian palaces with alcohol and friends we didn't meet in a Quake lobby was foreign to us. Our version of a jump shot involved a sniper rifle on an Xbox game, but now we drink with jocks.

We didn't have letters on our jackets before, and even though we still don't, we have the status that comes with it. It's crazy to think that high school can be separated by the letters on a jacket, but I've seen both sides, and to be completely honest I don't know which one I would rather live. Life wasn't as exciting before the bus, but it was certainly much simpler.

Before this nothing ever got between me and Derek. We had never argued. Ever. Something had changed. Was it me that had changed? Maybe.

"What we used to be," I repeated. She took it to mean I was agreeing with her, when in fact what I meant was something far beyond that. But I didn't elaborate that to her. Not yet. Not now.

I'd managed to avoid talking to my Mom about most of my social life pretty successfully, but she noticed when Derek stopped coming around the house as much. Before the accident, we basically lived at each other's houses at weekends. My Mom would often set an extra placemat at the dinner table for him. She would just assume that he would be there, and more often than not he was. The extra placemat stopped appearing shortly after he did. Mom asked me about it one day. She asked why he'd stopped coming round as much. She wanted to know if we'd fallen out or something. I told her, truthfully, that we both had our own stuff to deal with, and we just didn't have enough time to be messing around playing video games any more. I had Jenny and he had Dana.

I got out of Jenny's car and asked if she wanted to come in. She said she was probably going to go back to her house to sleep so she'd see me in the morning. Quietly I was thankful she wasn't coming in.

I went straight to my room after kissing Charlie on the forehead and laid down on my bed. My hand mindlessly wandered to the wallet in my pocket, looking for something to fiddle with to take my mind off Derek. The scratchcard was still in there, untouched.

Searching for something, anything, I could have control over, I reached into the wallet and found a coin. A nickel I walked over to my desk, sat down, and placed the card face up on the plywood. I touched the nickel to the card and paused, no longer sure. In a strange, inexplicable way, the only feeling that had remained constant throughout everything was my unknown curiosity for the scratchcard. It felt like a connector to my life before the accident. And I didn't want to lose that.

If this was the only constant left in my life, I was damn sure not going to destroy it any time soon. Putting it back in my wallet I sighed. That was the closest I had ever come to losing control and scratching it off. Anticipation or excitement didn't draw me to it today, it was something else. I couldn't control what happened with Derek or Dana or Jenny or even Charlie, but I could control the fate of the scratchcard, even if I couldn't control the outcome. But I didn't want to, I wanted to keep that connection, keep that constant, keep something the same as it used to be.

32

Derek still hadn't contacted me. Jenny promised me that he was going to get over it once Dana was out of hospital, but they were both in school on Monday and neither of them said anything to me, but Dana spoke to Jenny briefly at lunch. We were sat at our usual lunch table, expecting Dana and Derek to join us as normal, but they just walked straight past us with their lunch trays in hand. Jenny and I looked at each other in thought. She stood up and followed after them. I couldn't hear what was said but she told me when she returned.

"Derek doesn't want her talking to you, which, by association, means she can't talk to me, apparently," Jenny said.

"Why's he got a problem with you? You did nothing wrong."

"That's not strictly true. We both could have prevented anything from happening if we'd looked after her properly. But he isn't really mad at me. Dana isn't either. She isn't even mad at you, but Derek is still furious," she said. "Apparently."

"I don't…"

"I know, Alex," she said, cutting me off. "I don't either. Dana gets that it isn't our fault. She blames herself for not being more careful, but Derek won't listen to that logic, he needs someone to blame that's not her. And he can't blame the college guys because he doesn't know who they are yet. To be honest I think he blames himself more than anyone. He wasn't there to look after her, and the one time he wasn't there for her is when something bad happens. I think he's just projecting his anger on you, when it's himself he's angry at. Do you know why he wasn't there, by the way?"

I didn't know, I hadn't even asked what else he had planned. We were falling apart, falling away from each other. "He probably just has lots of studying to do. He can't wait to get away from this place," I said. That was true last time we'd spoken about college, at least. Maybe his decisions had changed since then. He was looking forward to getting out of his house and away from his parents and the rest of this town, just like I was. Maybe he'd changed his mind in the same way that I had. When my life changed, his did too. He came with me into this lifestyle and maybe he doesn't want to leave it behind either.

"Did she say anything else?" I asked.

"Not really, she just asked how I was, and how you were, et cetera."

Mason and his new girlfriend, Hayley, sat down opposite us. As usual, Mason's lunch tray was empty. He never bought anything but he always lined up in the queue anyway. He said that he loved the atmosphere of being with everybody in the queue, even though he hated the food they served at the end of it. He reached into his rucksack and grabbed the brown paper bag full of breaded chicken drumsticks that he would've picked up on his way into school.

"I still don't understand how you can eat them cold," Jenny said to him. We both watched as he tore strips of meat off the leg with his teeth.

"Listen here, toots," Mason said. 'Toots' was his new way of addressing people. "Do you think the very first caveman to discover that chicken was a tasty meal gave a crap whether it was hot or cold? He just wanted to get it down him so he had the energy and the strength to hide from a T-Rex."

"There are so many things wrong with that sentence, toots," Jenny said. "Firstly…"

"Don't bother," I butted in.

"Exactly," Mason said between bites. "Meowth's party was pretty fucking mental, don't you think?"

Jenny and I traded glances. Did he know what had happened?

"I don't actually remember seeing you there, Mace," I said. I didn't even know he went.

"Lost your memory of the night? It must have been a pretty good one then, am I right?" he proclaimed. "To be fair I just hung out in the pool with Hayley most of the night." He nudged Hayley in the ribs and winked at her. She giggled. "We were having a great time until some killjoy phoned the cops, weren't we Hale?" She giggled again. I'd met this girl a few times and I'd still never heard her communicate through anything other than giggles. "It was a legendary night though. For sure."

"I definitely won't forget it any time soon…" I agreed for completely different reasons.

"Damn right," Mason said. "Hey, why are the lovebirds eating on their Jackson Jones?" When we asked, he told us that was cockney for 'eating alone' and that I was the worst English Person he'd ever met. "Need some time by themselves, do they? They've been putty for each other since their date last week. It's cute. And sickening."

Date? I looked at Jenny for clarification, she looked back with a face that said: "Didn't you know?"

No. I didn't. I looked over to the table they were sat on. Something did look different between them. Before, their bodies would edge away from each other like magnets repelling, not able to make contact. Now they seemed relaxed. They were still magnets but one of them had flipped around and the attraction was blatant. I hadn't seen it before Mason mentioned it. Had it been like this for a while or was this only since Meowth's party? Derek should have told me about it. Surely he'd want advice on how to be on a first date, his first ever date. Although, did I ask him for advice when I went to Le Italiano with Jenny? I couldn't even remember.

"So are you up for Friday then?" Jenny said. My mind had wandered out of the conversation as I pondered Dana and Derek's date. My bemused expression wasn't the answer she was after.

"The playoff game, against Morrison High," Jenny elaborated. "You know, the massive school event that happens nearly every year. When we qualify for it, at least, the whole school turns up…"

"I've never been to one," I said.

"Oh yeah, you used to be a nobody," Mason said, and Jenny gasped. It took me by surprise as well. It was the first time any of us had addressed that. I didn't know what to say. "Oh come on it's not like we forgot," Mason said when I didn't reply. Hayley giggled, she was always fucking giggling. I glared at her.

"It'll be fun, toots," Mason continued. "Double-D will be there." He nodded towards the table where Derek and Dana were sat. "You two alright by the way? It seems like Batman and Robin haven't been spending as much time in each other's pockets as you used to." Mason was an idiot, but God dammit he was observant at times.

"Yeah, fine," I mumbled.

"So is that a yes then? Kick-off's at six," Jenny said, changing the subject, and I silently thanked her for doing so.

"Yeah sure, it will be fun, right?" I asked, unsure.

"Yeah it should be fun," she continued. "There will probably be an after party as well if we win people will want to get drunk and celebrate, and if we lose people will want to get drunk anyway."

"I'll come to the game, but I should probably skip the after party," I bargained. Adding "I really need to study" when they questioned me about it. Jenny looked at me knowingly, she knew that I wasn't going to be going anywhere near a party for a while.

At the other end of the cafeteria, Jordan sat with his friends, team-mates, fellow bullies, bastards and cronies. I didn't particularly want to spend my Friday night watching him be the king of the school once again, but I figured I should probably get involved in these school spirit things before I leave it behind.

The entire weekend was pretty much a write-off, studying wise, and I was behind on the schedule my Mom made for me. I bargained with myself that if I worked hard all week, I'd deserve a night off to relax with my friends. I just hoped for a quiet night.

33

By Friday I was ready to have a night off of studying. Nothing was getting in my way during the week so I filled every waking hour with books and words and numbers and facts and figures. It had overtaken my life just as fully and suddenly as when Jenny took over my life.

My routine for that week was entirely academic, so Friday came as both a reward and a break. Charlie pretty much spent the week in my room with me, he didn't have to take exams but he was studying with me anyway. I think he was just appreciating having me back at home. I'd spent more time at my house that week than I had for the entirety of the rest of the year.

He fell asleep in my bed on two nights. The first night I carried him back to his room and tucked him into his own bed, the second time I covered us both in my duvet and went to sleep with my hand on his.

Mom said no when I asked her if Charlie could come to the game with me and Mason. She said it was too dangerous for him to go on his own, and that it would be different if she or Dad came with us.

I didn't like the idea of sitting in front of my entire school with my parents, but when we got to the game, the place was full of parents and younger siblings.

Apparently, it's a massive family event. It seemed like the entire town was there. I almost felt bad for not inviting my parents. Almost.

Mason drove me to the match. Partly because he was the only person that could. Mom needed the car, Derek certainly wasn't going to be driving us and Jenny was already there, organising things.

Derek hadn't spoken to me all week. He was sticking to his word. Maybe if I apologised he would've dropped whatever problem he had with me and forget about it, but I wasn't going to apologise if he was going to be like this. I did miss him though.

The cheerleaders were warming up when we got there and Jenny was stood talking to them. She winked at me and I waved back at her. Before long she came to join us in the stands.

Derek and I had seen the cheerleaders practice, but we'd never seen a performance before. Mason had figured out that Derek was avoiding me, but that didn't seem to bother him and he sat down in the seats next to Derek and Dana.

"Move your bottle and glasses so we can sit down," Mason said to them.

He greeted them with gusto and they said hello. Derek didn't look at me but Dana glanced my way and smiled, it was a pure and sincere smile, not forced or faked and it made me feel better.

I felt awful for Dana, I hadn't even had a chance to make sure she was okay and tell her I was sorry I let her get in that situation. Something told me that she wouldn't accept my apology and would say something about how it was nobody's fault and we should all move on, I wished Derek shared the same views.

The blast of a cannon and the trill of a trumpet signalled that the performance was starting.

When they'd finished their routine the cheerleaders were replaced on the pitch by football players, girls jumping around in uniforms were replaced by boys jumping around in uniforms. I was not going to pretend that I understood anything about the rules of football, but to be honest, it didn't seem like many people in the crowd had a clue what was going on. Everyone just seemed to know when to cheer and when to hiss. Eventually, I got the hang of when crown participation was needed and when it wasn't.

Watching the cheerleaders and the footballers was not all that different, I didn't know what either set was doing but they were doing it well enough that I could see that they were doing it right. Unfortunately for Williamsburg, Morrison's team seemed to do everything a bit.

Morrison's players passed further, ran faster and tackled harder. We lost. I could tell that the crowd were deflated, but to me, it didn't matter at all. Going to the match was about getting out of the house and spending time with my friends. The score didn't change my plans for the day at all. Plus, my mood was lifted ever so slightly every time Jordan was hit with a crunching tackle. Like I said, Morrison tackled hard.

I wouldn't be going to the afterparty so if everyone was sad about the game it would be slightly less rowdy and I wouldn't have to worry as much about what would be happening there. In fact, I would say Williamsburg losing was the better result for me because I got to see Jordan upset.

Mason told me that scouts from the college he'd been accepted to were there to see him play. His offer depended on his footballing ability so he did everything he could to show it. In the end, though, it wasn't enough, and Williamsburg lost.

After the final whistle Jenny, Mason, Derek, Dana and I descended the stands to head to our respective cars. Jordan was the last player from our team left on the field. He was rolling the ball in his hands. He and I locked eye contact, and I deliberately grabbed Jenny's hand and turned my back to him. I provoked the bull and it saw red. I knew grabbing Jenny's would piss him off, but I couldn't resist.

It pushed him over the edge and when I turned back round to steal another glance at him I saw that the ball he was playing with wasn't in his hands anymore. It was hurtling through the sky towards my face.

I'd spent years throwing a baseball back and forth with Charlie and Derek. Catching a football couldn't be all that different from catching a baseball, surely? I had a split second to make my calculations before the ball hit me in the face. He'd thrown it hard.

Instantly, I made the decision to use this to my advantage. I adjusted my body position and plucked the ball out of the air inches from Jenny's face. She gasped. Derek, Dana and Mason turned around.

That was literally the manliest thing I'd done in my entire life so I was filled with adrenaline and testosterone. That, and a little bit of stupidity is what caused me to drop the ball and storm towards Jordan. The fifty yards between us felt like five and I was there in a flash. He towered over me in height and his already impressive bulk was added to by the armour he wore under his football jersey. His helmet was off so I could stare into his eyes, from below, but still, I tried my best to look intimidating. I don't think it worked.

"Judging by your performance in that game, I'm going to assume you were aiming for me, and your throw is just that bad that you nearly hit MY girlfriend instead," I said with extra emphasis.

"It was going straight at you, you jumped in front of her you little shit," Jordan spat back at me.

"If your aim was that good you probably wouldn't have lost," I said, I was coming dangerously close to having an argument about a sport I knew nothing about but I wanted to torment him a little bit and I knew losing would have pissed him off.

"Watch it," he growled, his height or weight or breadth didn't scare me anymore, because he may have the sporting ability and the physique and the scholarship, but I had the one thing that he didn't, and the one thing he wants most in the world.

Very deliberately, I turned to look at her. She was stood with Dana, Derek and Mason still, the look on each of their faces was identical. Bemusement, amazement, wonder, fear.

"Do you miss her?" I said as I turned back to Jordan. His lip was quivering and his fist was clenched, I was provoking him but I didn't care. I was not scared. I was strong. I was flying.

Literally.

Jordan's right fist connected with my jaw and knocked me off my feet, his left fist connected with my ribs before I hit the floor. He was on top of me as soon as my back connected with the grass that, just seconds before, was holding my feet up. Right before his right fist came crashing down on my skull I heard the shouts, after it connected I heard the stampede, and as his fist raised to throw another punch he was thrown onto his back by five or six players in football jerseys. Between them, they pinned him to the floor as I curled onto my knees and tried to stand up in a daze.

Whistles were blowing and I wondered if they were to signal the end of the game, but the game was over or I wouldn't have been on the field. Either the world was spinning more than it normally does or my head was. I suspected, and hoped, the latter; because a sudden increase in the world's axial rotation would have massive geological effects. That was when I realised I was concussed, and shortly after that, as the adrenaline and testosterone left my system in streams of my blood, I passed out.

34

Light filled the back of my eyelids as I woke up, but I did not open them. A quick self-diagnosis told me that I was largely unhurt, apart from the ringing in my head and the blood I could feel crusting beneath a plaster on my temple. Nothing was broken this time, so that was a plus. Voices talked over the buzzing that filled my head, familiar voices and one unfamiliar.

"How's your hand? Does it hurt?" I heard Mason say. I lay there confused. Was he talking to me? Why would my hand hurt? Maybe he was talking to Jordan, his hand would hurt from the number of my bones it had just come into contact with, but why would Jordan be here, wherever "here" is? My lips opened to answer with my eyes still closed but another familiar voice answered before I could. My lips closed again.

"Fucking hurts. Seriously, the things I do for him," I heard Derek say. That made me even more confused. Although, I had just been knocked out so I shouldn't be too hard on myself for being a bit slow on the uptake. Why was Derek's hand hurting? I asked myself. Did Jordan hit him too? But why would he punch him on the hand? My mind filled itself with questions and when they didn't find any answers they forced themselves from my lips. I opened my eyes.

"Who… what… why… Where am I?" I blurted out and my eyes darted around the room trying their best to answer some of my brain's questions. I could see where I was but I didn't know where that was. White walls surrounded me, it looked like a prison cell, and the long reclining chair I was led on made it feel more like a dentist's office. Neither of those guesses was right.

"The nurse's office," said the voice that I had been waiting to hear. I turned and faced her and there was the blue I knew so well, the blue washed across me like the ocean and woke me up.

"Surely you've been here before."

I hadn't. The place was foreign to me, I didn't recognise it. This was not the first time something like this had happened to me but it was the first time I'd ended up in the nurse's office for it. Shouldn't there be a nurse in the nurse's office? I wondered without speaking.

"Whose hand hurts?" I said, looking into the faces of the people around me. Along with the voices I'd heard, voices of Derek and Jenny and Mason, Dana was here, and so was Daniel Marks in a Williamsburg school football jersey. He still had his under armour on. I flinched as I looked at him, a reflex from the last time I saw a football jersey.

"It's cool man," he said, raising both his palms in the air towards me. He'd noticed my recoil and was showing me he was unarmed, he was safe. He was safety.

"Dan was the one that ripped Jordan off of you," Mason explained. "After Derek lamped him that is. Jordan gave Dan a kick to the stomach on his way down."

My mind lost control of my eyes and they flashed from Derek to Daniel to Mason to Jenny and back again. Derek had one hand on the back of Dana's chair, and the other was wrapped in a bandage in his lap. Daniel was stood against the wall with his hands outstretched. Jenny was sat closest to me.

"I'm alright," Daniel said as he noticed me look towards his stomach, "He knocked the wind out of me so coach said I needed to get checked out."

My head nodded without me telling it to and pain surged through my skull.

"No sudden movements, Alex," said a new voice from the doorway. A woman, who I assumed was the nurse, stood there with bandages in her hand.

"Yes ma'am," I said, reflexively.

"Daniel, you're free to go," the nurse said. "I've just been to check in with your coach and cleared you to leave. They're waiting for you out front."

"Right, that's my cue then I guess," Daniel said and made to walk out, our eyes met as he hovered by the door. "Glad you're alright."

"Thanks for jumping in like that, you really didn't have to," I said.

"Oh yes I did. You did the same for me, remember? It wasn't just me. A few of the guys helped me hold him down. We've all had enough of Jordan's shit," Daniel said. "I'm just glad you're alright."

"So am I," Jenny and I said in unison.

"See you around," Daniel said, and he left.

"And you?" I said, turning to Derek. "What happened to you? You "lamped" Jordan?" Mason laughed as I quoted him.

"Kinda," Derek said. "At least I think I did, I've never thrown a punch before so I didn't really know what I was doing. I managed to sprain my wrist somehow. His skull probably did more damage to my wrist than the other way round."

All I could do was laugh. Words escaped me. We all laughed, and even when the laughing hurt I carried on laughing because it was good to laugh with Derek again. It had been so long. When the laughter died I had a question for Derek, a simple one.

"Why?"

"You would've done the same for me," he said. And he was right. "I realised that you do care for someone else, other than yourself. You wouldn't have squared up to him like that if you didn't. It was selfless. It was idiotic, but it was selfless, standing up for her like that." And he nodded towards Jenny.

"I swear you're always here when I wake up," I said to her. "Not that I'm complaining."

She smiled.

"So yeah, I hit him and that kind of shocked him more than it hurt him I think," Derek said. "It stopped him for just long enough for Dan to pile drive him off you. It was literally better than any tackle in the whole of the football game itself, but he took a knee to the stomach and he was puffing like mad for a bit after. Then when his teammates had caught up with him they dog piled on top of Jordan because he was trying to get up. Man, I know it's a bad situation and everything but it was hilarious watching it. Jordan's friends tried to help but I don't think they wanted to do anything to piss off Jordan. He basically owns them."

"Oh shit, that reminds me," Mason said. "Jordan lost his scholarship."

"WHAT?" the rest of us said at once. We all looked to Mason for answers.

"Yeah, Alex, after they'd taken you in on a stretcher I saw Jordan talking to the guys in the suits and Headmaster Chang," he continued. "You know the scouts were here to see him play? I guess the scout saw what happened between you and him. Well, his scholarship had a behavioural clause, didn't it? They only want perfect students in their college, no troublemakers. The scout told him his scholarship was now void. He went crazy. A few of the Morrison guys had to restrain him again. I don't even know where he is now. I came right here to check on you."

"Wow." That was all I could say. I'd thought about what I could do to take that scholarship away from him, but I'd decided he didn't deserve it. I thought we were done. But in the end, he took it away from himself.

35

After the game, and after 'the fight', as everyone was calling it, things quietened down again. Calling it a fight implied a few things that were completely untrue about what happened. First, to me at least, a conventional fight involves two people throwing arms, legs, elbows and heads at each other, basically anything that's solid enough to hurt someone. That was not what this was. I didn't throw any limb or appendage in Jordan's general direction, mainly because I knew any attempt I made to hurt him would've been futile. As proven by Derek's sprained wrist.

Secondly, fights are supposed to last longer than two punches, right? The way it had been described in hallways and classrooms since it happened made it seem like it was an epic battle that spanned hours, not a few seconds as it really was.

Thirdly, stories were told of Jordan wiping out three Morrison players just to get to me before Derek threw himself in front of Jordan's raging fist as he tried to impale me on it. When in reality it was a sucker punch and pretty solid jab to the ribs that wiped me out, the fracas and hurrah came after I was unconscious.

My notoriety in the school was at an all-time high, bigger than when I jumped in front of the bus. Maybe it was because I was already known in the school now, or maybe it was because everyone had respect for the kid who took on Jordan. What caused the most outrage among students was that Jordan faced no retrospective punishment from the school, because technically it happened after school hours and not on school grounds. The football pitch belongs to the town council, not the school. Everyone knew, or at least assumed, that the reason the school's hands were tied on the situation was that Jordan's Dad was on the board of governors, and he invested heavily into the football team.

He may not have been kicked out of school but his scholarship was definitely gone. After Mason told me about it, it was all anyone could talk about. Playing football was the entire and only reason Jordan was going to college. That and frat parties, I'd imagine.

He was back at Williamsburg on Monday morning, but his strut around campus was different than before. He was no longer the admirable captain of Williamsburg's finest football team for generations. Now he was a degenerate thug who people feared. He was feared before, but this is a different type of fear. People were scared of him before because of his social and physical stature, he was the kingpin of our school. Now, if you will, he was more King Kong. Unpredictable and violent. He'd become an outcast in the school, and nobody wanted to go near him. Even his teammates shied away from him.

Of the many occasions, I had been beaten up by Jordan, this was definitely my favourite. Because now it wasn't a dirty little secret that I had to keep to myself, this was something the whole school knew about, and they were all on my side. Would it have been like this if people knew about it back then? I couldn't answer my own question.

The after party that had been planned for after the game was cancelled. Most of the school had seen what had happened on the field. Mobs had gathered when they saw me square up to him. It was like when you drive past a car crash on the highway, you know that what's happened is awful, but you can't help but look when you drive past it. The party was going to be at Daniel's house but he called it off because of what happened. After I left the nurse's office that night and Mason had left to go back to his house, the four of us went to Ed's Diner and just stayed there the entire night. We fed each other fries and sipped on our milkshakes for hours, we laughed and joked because the four of us were back together. We'd put everything behind us and we were whole again.

Derek had forgiven me for not looking after Dana and part of me thinks that's because he'd forgiven himself as well. In that diner we were finally able to talk alone about everything we'd missed, even though Jenny and Dana were with us we could still talk like we used to. He spoke freely about his date with Dana, saying "yeah it was alright." Dana threw a French fry at him. Together, they spoke about how their relationship had progressed in secret, and they even thanked me for bringing them together. Without Jenny and me they wouldn't have found each other, and they are so glad that they did. And I am too.

Everything I'd done to get to that point in my life had paid off. I was thankful for the times before things changed, because if they'd been any different I might not have thrown myself in front of a bus to save the life of the girl I love. I'm thankful that repeatedly saving Jenny was enough to make her love me, I don't feel bad that I had to lie to her just to keep her by my side because right then, in that booth in that diner I was complete, and without all the things I had done in my life and all the choices I had made, good or bad, I would not have been in that situation, on that table, with that girl.

36

That Friday night in Ed's, Jenny reminded me of another school tradition, the end of year awards. 'A little bit of fun before your exams start' is how the faculty describe. Nobody ever took it seriously, and the awards didn't really mean anything. The entire student body gathers in our auditorium for the first, last and only time that year on the final Friday before finals start, the Friday a week after the play-off game. There were no lessons that day. The entire day was taken over by the awards ceremony. They give out awards for academic achievement during the year.

It never made sense to me to give that award out before exams, but the school knew they would never get seniors to sit through it after exams when they'd technically finished at the school. Other awards given out would be for sporting recognition and things of a similar ilk, Jordan was going to get an award because he had led his team to the playoffs, Dana was getting an award because of her contribution to the tutoring scheme.

Jenny dropped the bomb on me Monday morning that I would also be getting an award. Principal Chang had called her into his office during first period and discussed the idea of giving me one. "What for?" I asked her. We were stood at my locker in the break between classes. Names and faces passed by us as people rushed to class.

"'Heroics in the face of danger,'" she said, laughing. "The bus."

"Are you kidding?" I said. "You told him not to bother, right?"

"Yes, of course. But he thought I was just being modest. He said you deserve it for setting a shining example of the school."

"Plus he loved the amount of media coverage it got him," Derek said. He and Dana had joined us before our next class started.

"What does getting an award involve?"

"You have to sit on the stage with the other awardees until you get your award," Dana answered. "It's a huge drag but it looks good on college applications and stuff."

"Awardees?" Derek asked. "Is that even a word? You're supposed to be getting an award for tutoring the dumb kids and you're just making up words?"

"Actually yes, it is a word..." Dana said. She blinked a lot when she spoke. I'd never noticed that before. "And the fact you don't know that probably shows why I'm getting one and you aren't," she jibed. "Maybe you could do with some tutoring."

Derek looked hurt so she reached up and kissed him on the cheek. They didn't mind showing their affection in public now, they were now an official 'thing' not just a 'thing' when they were drunk. To begin with, I pretended to vomit when they were like this, but after Derek reminded me that he had to put up with Jenny and I doing the exact thing I conceded he had a point and let them be. It was good to see my best friend like this anyway.

—

Those of us who were receiving awards were given two extra tickets to the ceremony so our parents could come. It was on a Friday so Dad couldn't afford to take the day off work so Mom and Charlie came to watch, Mom still hadn't got a job. To be honest, I think even if Dad was able to come, Charlie would still get the ticket over him. He was so excited when I told him about it.

"Charlie," I signed to him. **"You and Mom are going to come to see me get an award from my school on Friday. Does that sound like something you'd want to do?"**

"What's the award for?" he signed back. His hands moved quickly, excitedly.

"Do you remember when I saved Jenny from getting hurt and I got hurt myself?" I said, putting it simply for him. **"Well, the school wants to award me for that."**

"Wow. You're like a real-life superhero!"

"Something like that," I said out loud.

As I looked out into the crowd on Friday afternoon I could see him and Mom in their seats near the front.

The auditorium had tiered seating like they have in cinemas, I felt like I was the one on show. There were twelve of us in total, including Dana for her tutoring, and Jordan and his football team vice-captain. Because Jenny would be graduating soon, they chose today to announce the new student council president. Her replacement, Lorna, had a chair too. I wondered how Jenny had got out of getting an award for everything she does. The rest of the chairs were for the people at the top of each academic field, they were all seniors apart from one sophomore whose name tag read 'Sarah, History.'

The name tag on my chair was originally in the first of the two rows of chairs but I swapped with 'James, Maths' for his seat in the back row. No way did I want to be at the front. I noticed that where I was supposed to sit was at the complete opposite end of the row to Jordan's chair. They clearly wanted to keep us apart.

The whole ceremony was about more than the twelve awards they were going to be giving out, it was about celebrating our achievements as a school and looking towards the future. Unity and togetherness was a common theme from the various speakers Principal Chang had called in to talk to us.

The first speaker was Mrs Commons, head of academics at Williamsburg. She spoke about how each and every subject is as important as the other, and that the faculty had worked together to make that clear. She said that the reason the people on this stage have achieved what they did is that they worked together. I didn't really understand this link but I got what she was trying to say.

One by one she beckoned the academic achievers to her to collect their awards. They did so in an organised fashion that we had been forced to practice for an hour before the guests arrived. After they'd collected their awards they were told to go and join their friends in the audience. This was Principal Chang's personal touch, he said that joining their peers showed unity in itself.

The second speaker was Dr Stevenson, the admissions supervisor at Kansas University. He spoke to the crowd about how one of the things that they look for, even above grades, when they go through college applications is extracurricular activities. They love applicants who have shown they have a desire to help the school around them. This was when he told the school that Lorna would be Jenny's successor as student council president. There was a brief cheer from a few parts of the crowd when Jenny's name was mentioned, and I was tempted to join in.

Stevenson said he looked forward to seeing Lorna at KU in the future, and she left the stage and joined her friends in the audience. The chairs around me were emptying fast, I could no longer hide behind the people sat in front of me. Just Dana, Jordan, his vice-captain and I remained seated on stage.

Dr Stevenson continued his speech by saying how he and his college admired people who were willing to take time to help others. With this, he beckoned Dana towards him and explained how people like her, people that tutored and helped others, were an inspiration to those around her. She accepted her award and left the stage to join the audience. I didn't know where they were sat; I lost sight of Dana as soon as she left the stage. The lights blaring down on the stage blinded me and made me sweat. I hoped it wasn't noticeable. I was sweating even more now that Dana had gone. I knew it was my turn after her.

All I could see in the crowd was the front row, where Charlie and Mom were sat. She was moving her hands as fast as she could, translating everything the speakers were saying so Charlie wouldn't miss anything. Only then did I realise how much my Mom had given up looking after Charlie. She was missing the entire presentation because she was busy making sure he didn't miss anything. That summed up my Mom. Ever since Charlie's accident, looking after him was her top priority. She gave up a job that she loved to make sure he had an education. She never went out with her friends anymore, not like she used to. My Mom used to be so sociable, but Charlie has taken up her entire life. Looking at Charlie and my Mom calmed me down. I wished I could see Jenny among the faces in the crowd. I needed to see blue again.

Dr Stevenson went on to say that there was another amongst the awardees who gave himself to help others. I smiled at the thought of Dana elbowing Derek in acknowledgement because the speaker had said 'awardees'. I saw Charlie's face light up as he figured out that my moment was coming up. I winked at him and he waved and it made everything better. If only for a second.

"Alex Morgan…" he began. My head perked up. I wasn't ready yet. Thankfully he continued before calling me up. "…showed unbelievable awareness, self-sacrifice and bravery to do what he did in early September. In case some of you in the audience don't know, Alex here…" and this time he did point to me, but I still wasn't ready to stand up. "…saved the life of one of his fellow students at the start of this academic year." A few gasps were audible from the one percent of the crowd that hadn't heard this story. "A female student stepped into the road without seeing an oncoming bus, but Alex chased after her, knocked her out of the way of the bus, and took the hit from the bus himself…" there were a few more gasps, maybe even a cheer, but the room was silent apart from that. "…he was hospitalised and was put on crutches, but I'm happy to say he fought through it, with the help of his peers, and he's here to collect this award from me today. Alex, if you would come forward please."

I stood up. I walked across the stage. Four foot felt like four hundred foot. It was the longest and slowest walk of my life. It felt like I was walking the green mile to my execution. This was supposed to be a celebration but I felt unhinged and nervous. The audience started to cheer, which relaxed me a little bit. Charlie was on his feet clapping, so were a few others. I shook the doctor's hand as he handed me my award. It was a glass plaque: modern looking, transparent but solid. The words "Alex Morgan: Heroics in the face of danger." were inscribed on it, I tried to hold it up high, to show my thanks, but my arms were too weak to hold it much higher than chest height. My eyes scanned the crowd for Jenny as I walked to the stairs leading to the audience. I had made it through that experience relatively unscarred, people were even cheering.

But then, the cheering stopped and some people gasped.

I stopped.

When I turned around, my vision was blurry, the lights blinding. My eyes focused and I saw Jordan, stood in the middle of the stage, taking the microphone from Dr Stevenson.

This was not in the plan.

This was not in the script.

Jordan opened his mouth and spoke clearly and concisely. He'd practised this speech.

37

"Ladies and Gentleman, honoured guests, my fellow students... If I may, I have something to add to Doctor Stevenson's words. His description of Alex Morgan's heroics earlier this year was accurate, and quite touching. But I just had to add something myself.

"Alex, I've never said this to you before, but I want to thank you for saving my girlfrie—well, I guess she's your girlfriend now. You've saved her on many occasions this year, actually. Some of you in the crowd may not know this, but the bus incident was not Alex's only heroic act this year. Yes, yes, I know, shocking isn't it? Our very own knight in shining armour has saved his damsel in distress more than once this year. Isn't that wonderful? Shortly after he saved her from the bus, he saved her again.

"He and Jenny were at the mall when a hooded thug ripped Jenny's purse from her hands and ran off. Alex, the hero that he is, tore after the guy and took him down with a tackle that wouldn't look out of place on our football pitch. I was there, and I saw the whole thing. I saw Alex tackle the thief and retrieve Jenny's handbag and I saw the mugger get up and run off as Alex returned his girlfriend's bag. How brave.

"His next act was almost an exact replication of the first one. Alex and Jenny were stood at the front of the school – in exactly the same place as that first time, with the bus – when suddenly a car appeared, drove right through a puddle, and swerved onto the pavement towards them. Alex repeated his actions from September and pulled Jenny out of the way of the vehicle. It wasn't quite as dramatic this time, but he saved her again. It was becoming a habit.

"And he had more in him. Believe it or not, he even managed two in one night. Alex found himself the hero again at Meo—Asmir's party. As a drunken sophomore stumbled at the top of a flight of stairs, over a sizable gentleman, Alex grabbed his girlfriend and pulled her to safety as the fat lard landed on his back in the exact spot she'd just been standing. I saw it happen and his reaction times were fantastic – it was almost like he knew it was going to happen. Later that night he saved someone else when he found Dana Jalofski unconscious in a bedroom with a random college guy. Alex immediately called the cops, and it didn't matter to him that he was drunk underage, or on drugs, he just wanted to make sure his friend was okay, so he phoned the police. And, thankfully, everyone turned out okay.

"Alex's most recent heroic act was one I'm sure a lot of you in this room remember. After last week's playoff game, Alex caught a ball that I threw at him. I threw it hard. I won't lie and say that I didn't throw it with the intention of smacking him in his pathetic little face. But apparently my aim was slightly off, and the ball flew towards Jenny's face instead. Alex caught the ball before it hit her, and then he squared up to me to defend her honour. Very noble. I almost felt bad about knocking him the fuck out.

"But he had it coming, and I'd been waiting for my moment. Because Alex, I've been watching you. I've been waiting for you to slip up. And you did. And I can think of no better opportunity than this to reveal the truth about you. You see, everyone, of the times I have just described where Alex was the hero, only one of them was real. Only the first one. The rest are events that happened, sure, but Alex was not the hero he made himself out to be, not the hero everyone made him out to be.

"The time in the shopping centre? The mugger? The mugger was a friend of Alex's. Yeah, yeah, settle down. The mugger and Alex arranged the whole thing, I know because I followed the mugger after he left the scene and I saw his face. Who was it? It was Derek Windhurst. And who was driving the car that almost hit him and Jenny? Derek Windhurst. His hood was up, but I saw him. Maybe he thought everyone would be looking in Alex's direction, wondering what the hero had done this time. But I saw Derek drive off, hood up, head down. Alex even engineered the thing with the kid and the fat guy at that party, just for an excuse to save Jenny's ass again. Knowing Alex, he probably spiked Dana's drink himself just so he could pop up and be the hero again.

"When I knew for sure Alex was a fake I didn't speak up right away. I waited. Waited until my voice could properly be heard, until everyone could know the truth. I lost my temper last week when he made it look like the ball was going to hit Jenny. I never miss. I just don't. I know in my heart that that throw was going, but he angled himself to make it look like I'd aimed for Jenny. It wasn't. I know it wasn't. And I would never EVER hurt her.

Now though, it's time. Time for all of this. Time that you all heard the truth about your hero and saviour."

38

My life fell.

I don't know how long I stood there, staring at Jordan from below the stage. His speech was meticulous. He'd planned every word to do the maximum damage he could, and it worked. And he was right about almost everything.

I could feel the hostility around me. I could feel the stares from the crowd. I couldn't turn around and face them. During his speech, I heard, rather than saw, what was going on in the audience behind me. The gasps and shouts told me that people felt conned. They'd built me up to be a hero, and that hero worship was built on a foundation of lies. My relationship was built on lies. Without turning around, I knew that Jenny was looking at me the entire time.

Without thought, I climbed the steps I had just descended and returned to the stage. Jordan moved out of the way of the podium in centre stage. He'd set the microphone to his height. I adjusted it to be level with my mouth. I scanned the crowd and found Charlie. He looked confused. Mom must have stopped translating when Jordan started speaking. I didn't look at her. I couldn't bear it. I looked right at Charlie. To him, I was still a hero. He didn't hear what had just been said, and in that moment he still idolised me. With no words of my own in mind, nothing planned, I looked into Charlie's eyes and started speaking.

"You're all looking at me like I'm a monster… The funny thing is that at the start of the year barely any of you knew who I was. I was just another brick in the wall. Ironically, the only person that knew me is the one person that's put me in this situation. Jordan is a dick who has ruined my life. He's probably going to kill me, and he may as well because there's not much more he can do to me now.

Jordan beat me up for years. Tormented and abused me, physically and emotionally. It started in third grade. It didn't just happen on the field last week. And now he's finally finished me off.

"I could stand here and deny everything he's just said, and say it was just his way of getting revenge for the fact I made him lose his scholarship, but I won't. Because almost everything he said was true.

"Do any of you have any idea what it was like for me before I jumped in front of that bus? You can sit there and judge me for doing the best I could to fit in, but just stop and think for a minute. If you had treated me differently, hell, even just treated me like I existed, then maybe I wouldn't need to jump in front of a bus to get you all to notice me. And I wouldn't have to do everything else just so I didn't lose your attention.

"I feel I owe some people an explanation, but to the rest of you, I owe nothing. You gave me no time before things changed so I'll give you no time now that they've changed back.

"Jenny. Jenny… There are too many people in this room and the lights are too bright and I have no idea where you are, but this is to you. I don't regret saving your life at all. Because the world is a better place with you in it. I've been in love with you for years and when we got together I was so worried about not being good enough for you that I tried too hard to keep you. In reality, all I did was push you away by lying to you. I was desperate and scared, so I flipped out. I felt inferior to you in every way, not because of anything you did... It's just... you're Jenny fucking Evans for fuck sake. When I felt I was losing you, I thought I needed to impress you to keep you, and the only way I could think of to do that was to create these fake situations where I could save you, where I could be your hero again... Because without that, I felt like I was nothing. Not enough. And then everything just escalated, I had to carry on trying to keep you interested, and like a runaway train on a broken track, everything just got out of control, and it went too far.

"Dana, wherever you are, I want you to know that what Jordan suggested—that I spiked your drink to make myself the hero again—that's wrong. I'd never put you in danger like that, and I'm so glad you're okay. Yes, I was desperate to be 'cool' or, but I would never put you in danger. Ever. And please know that Derek only went along with it all because that's the type of person he is. He wanted me to be happy whatever it took, and he knew what I was willing to do to get there. The rest of you probably don't realise why I felt the need to create this fake persona of a hero, or whatever you want to call it, but I'll try to explain in the only way I know how...

"Derek, where are you, you'll know what I mean... it's like you're playing a video game and you know the cheat codes. Cheats make you invincible, or level you up much faster, or double in size. Well, that's what I felt like after saving Jenny from that bus. To begin with, I was scared about coming back to school, but the way everyone treated me when I got back made me feel untouchable. Like I'd doubled in size. Like I was invincible. And once you've lived with invincibility you never want to go back to being breakable.

"I'll admit, I loved it. I loved being cool and I loved going to parties and I love the new friends I've made, but I was scared of losing it. So I started thinking of situations I could create that would make me seem like the good guy again. I wanted to be the hero you all wanted me to be. To begin with, it was just a thought, but I got so scared that I was going to lose everything I flipped out and faked a mugging, then I faked the thing with the car, and yeah I faked the thing on the stairs at Meowth's.

"The way she looked at me after I saved her from the bus… that's why I carried on doing it. The friends and the parties were good, but none of it compared to how it made me feel when Jenny looked me in the eyes and told me that she loved me."

39

I had to get out. I walked away from the podium and down the steps, not stopping for anyone. Charlie got out of his seat and turned to follow me but Mom held him back. She was crying.

Derek stood up. He was holding Dana's hand. At least I knew the two of them were going to be okay and that I hadn't ruined that as well. Derek opened his mouth to say something but no words came.

On the other side of Derek, I saw the blonde hair that I knew was Jenny's, but I couldn't bear to look at her.

A few people jeered as I made my way down the aisle, something hit me on the back of the leg but I didn't stop to look what it was. This feeling wasn't like before. Back then nobody noticed me enough to hurl abuse at me, nobody knew me well enough to dislike me. Now everybody knew me. Everybody hated me.

When I reached the front entrance to the school I saw the rain. It must have started during the award ceremony. I thought back to when it rained and I saved Jenny from the car. Except I didn't save her, not that time. I conned her. I conned everyone. I thought back to when it was raining and we kissed under the umbrella and on the bridge above the pond. I thought of the waterfall and I finally knew why it had always felt like a metaphor for something.

Water crashed down on water. It crashed down on itself. It sucked water into the system, raised it all the way to the top, and then sent it crashing down to the bottom. It was stuck in a cycle, but never going anywhere.

Other people could hurt me, Jordan had proved that, but no one could ever do as much damage to me as I'd done to myself. I knew that now.

I open the doors and step out into the rain, marching away from the school without direction, wanting to be anywhere other than that auditorium. If I walk far enough, for long enough, no one would remember what happened. No one would remember me.

Looking for a distraction I reach inside the wallet in my back pocket and grab the scratchcard.

It's still untouched. The rain is pelting down, making the card wet. It's becoming flimsy. Fumbling around in my wallet for a nickel I cut my thumb on the zip. A small cut appears with a tiny amount of blood. I lick my thumb to get rid of the blood and it goes away at first but then another droplet of blood replaces it.

I lick it again and the blood stays away for a little longer, but again it comes back. A drop of rain lands on the cut and mixes with the blood.

After finally retrieving a coin from my wallet, I place the scratchcard on the back of my left wrist and hold it in place with the heel of my right. Between the thumb and first finger of my hand, I hold a nickel, and begin to scratch. The latex film peels off under the force of the coin.

The first number revealed is $75,000.

I stop walking, and put all my concentration into discovering my fate. There are six numbers to be revealed in total, and I need to match three to win that amount. The second number revealed under the latex film is $250. My hand is steadying now, determined to finish what I started. Thirdly, $250 is revealed. Only one more $250 to win something. Three down, three to go. $15,000 is the fourth number revealed.

I look up before revealing the penultimate number, but no one is around. I scratch.

It's $75,000 again.

I think of what $75,000 could do for Charlie. He could go to a school that caters for the deaf and he could make real friends, and Mom could go back to work and take the burden off of Dad. One more $75,000 could change everything. I place the coin down and start to scratch off the last bit of latex. I get as far as the dollar sign when I hear a shout.

"ALEX!"

I can't take any more ridicule. I close my eyes and scratch away the last square.

"ALEX WAIT!"

Jenny.

It's Jenny's voice.

Everything I've done was in a quest to make her mine and keep it that way, but now she's going to hate me. She's going to tell me that I'm pathetic and worthless and that she is far too good for me.

She screams.

"Alex, I— ALEX LOOK OUT."

She screams because she sees it.

She screams because this time I don't see it.

This time I don't see it until it's too late.

I don't see it until I open my eyes and decide to turn back.

I start to turn towards her, and that's when I see it.

In that frozen moment, I understand why the dog didn't move. My brain shouts move, Jenny shouts move, but my feet don't react.

A whisper escapes my lips but the rest of my body is paralysed. She's getting closer and closer to me. It's getting closer and closer to us. She reaches me and one of us reacts, my mind is frozen but my body is able. I look into her eyes and there is blue for the last time.

The last word I ever speak to Jenny Evans is an echo of the first one I said to her.

38293563R00141

Printed in Poland
by Amazon Fulfillment
Poland Sp. z o.o., Wrocław